CW01457638

Ebook ISBN: 978-1-951968-25-0

Print ISBN: 978-1-951968-26-7

# GET YOUR FREE STORY!

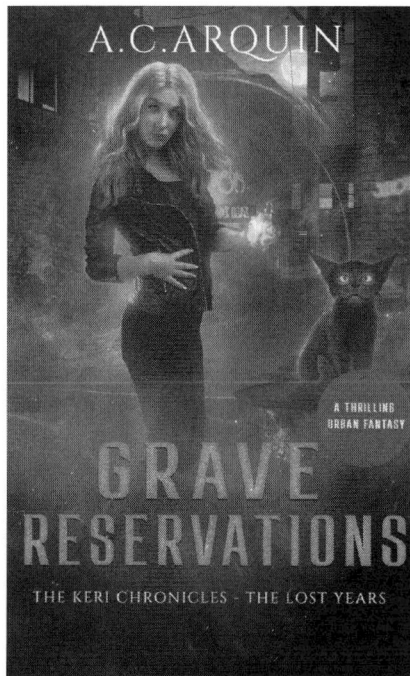

*Join the Arquinworlds Reader Group to get your free story from The Keri Chronicles - The Lost Years! Go to www.arquinworlds.com.*

# BLACK RAIN

## THE KERI CHRONICLES

### A.C. ARQUIN

# 1

R osa woke with a scream. She jolted upright in the close air of her bedroom, panting, sheets knotted around her limbs. Heart pounding in the dark. Hair sweat-plastered to her head.

The dreams were getting worse.

Lightning flashed through the window, sizzling from cloud to cloud like a living thing. Restless and questing, never still for a moment. A fleeting touch, gone as quickly as it arrived.

She and the darkened sky sat silent. The world held its breath.

Thunder crashed, rolling along behind the spark, heavy waves behind the tide. Shaking the walls of her bedroom, it roared on and on, louder than all the bells in all the cathedrals in all the world pealing at once. So fierce even the bedrock cowered beneath the barrage.

Rosa screamed again, her voice lost in the roar.

Finally the sound trailed away, leaving a deep vibration in her bones. A restless itching. An unquietness in the dark.

She made her way to the bathroom, limbs shaking, the dream playing over and over in her mind.

*The man sat on the Golden Gate bridge, gazing down at the water. Rain fell in sheets, nearly obscuring the lights of the city, twinkling in the distance. So many lives in tidy little boxes. Shining in the dark.*

*But not his.*

*His hair was wet, soaked strands heavy upon his forehead. Rivulets of water ran down the back of his neck. The water was cold, even colder than the air around him. For once the wind wasn't blowing. At least there was that.*

*The man noticed none of this. His eyes were fixed on the water. The falling water and the gray water far below. The restless channel where the bay and the Pacific Ocean collided, churning currents vying for dominance.*

*People came to the Golden Gate to kill themselves. To climb over the rail and leap down into that frigid water. Hundreds of them every year. Maybe thousands. The man didn't know the statistics, didn't particularly care. The only number that mattered to him was the number that transfixed every person who sat where he sat. The number one.*

*One life.*

*Full of pain.*

*One life so unbearable that the only way out was down.*

*This, the man understood.*

*The rain fell steadily, as it had every day for weeks. The downpour never stopped. There were no bright days, no blue sky, no warmth on his face and neck. Only the rain, cold and unrelenting.*

*The rain had been here long before people first colonized these shores. Before they came with wooden boats and axes. Lighting their sad little fires in a vain attempt to keep the chill at bay.*

*The people were a fleeting spark, less than the blink of an eye. The rain was eternal. It cared nothing for the small humans, hardly noticing them.*

*The rain was calling to him.*

*It was time to stop grasping at the spark of life. Time to stop tending the fire.*

*Time to let go and join the rain.*

*He gripped the rail and heaved himself up, hauling his body over the barrier with surprising strength.*

*Balanced on the rail, he gazed out at the city one last time. He couldn't see the lights anymore. The clouds had swallowed them whole.*

*Which was fine. The light was a lie anyway. A worthless facade. People were not light and good. Life was pain and darkness and wickedness.*

*The rain turned to blood as he clenched his hand into a fist. Soon all of that would be gone, too. The rain would cleanse the city. Cleanse the world.*

*He let go, and the storm took him home.*

Rosa staggered down the hall on bare feet, lightning flashes creating stepping stones in the dark. She turned on the bathroom tap by feel, splashing cold water over her feverish face. Stood there trembling.

The dream hung heavy and vivid across her mind. Lightning and thunder. Despair and anger. The man's hands red with blood.

And over it all: rain. Rain that never stopped. Dark water rising like a biblical flood. Rising to swallow the city whole.

This was the third time she'd dreamt of the shadowy figure, and it had been the worst one yet. She didn't know how or why, but she knew that people were going to die. Beyond the sadness and rage there was a coldness to the figure. Like death walking the earth.

Rosa glanced at the clock. Four a.m. She sighed. It could have been worse. Sometimes the dreams woke her at one or two. Four was practically a full night's sleep.

She padded through the silent flat to the kitchen and put the kettle on, the ancient hardwood floor cold against the bottom of her feet. She'd been living on tea for weeks, unable to keep anything else down. Her stomach twisted with nausea at the mere thought of food.

She hadn't been eating, hadn't been sleeping. She could feel herself wasting away, consumed by the visions.

Yet she couldn't bring herself to care.

The worst part was that, even though she couldn't make out his features, Rosa was sure that she knew the man in the dream. If she could only figure out who he was, maybe she could stop the dreams' predictions from coming true.

Because they were predictions. She knew it in her bones. The things in the dreams hadn't happened yet.

But they would.

She felt the truth of it in her soul. The dreams were true visions. Why they'd been sent to her was irrelevant. The important question was: What was she going to do with them?

She reached for the kitchen light. Flicked it on.

And screamed again.

In the reflection of the kitchen window, Rosa saw herself, pale, thin and disheveled. Her face and hands were covered in blood.

# 2

"**F**ucksocks!" Valora Keri dropped the hammer and danced around the living room, shaking her thumb.

In her head, Mister E snorted. *"It's a good thing building things is not part of your magical repertoire. Any golems you created would look like a kindergartener's stick drawing."*

"You could help instead of criticizing."

*"Oh, no. I really couldn't. I don't have a corporeal body, remember?"* The demon cat was lying on a pillow in the window seat, but he floated a couple of feet in the air above it to emphasize his point. *"Besides, cats hate hammers. If you think your thumb hurts, you should try hitting your tail with one of those things."*

Val waved the tool at him. "Maybe I will."

Mister E floated out of reach, his striped gray tail dropping down as he turned onto his back.

*"Seriously, though, deconstruction is the easy part. If you're crushing your thumbs while knocking out the walls, just wait until you actually have to put nails into boards."*

"You have no idea how much I'm looking forward to that," she said, glaring at the pair of petrified gray fingers on her left hand. They made manual labor awkward, to say the least. "Whose idea was this again?"

"I'm pretty sure it was yours," Malcolm came breezing into the room, holding a trio of steaming mugs. He handed one to Val and the other to Sandra, who was prying out the scorched baseboard molding below the boarded-up windows. "Now sit down and drink this coffee before you hurt yourself again. We already had to go visit Alice yesterday. I'm sure the poor homeless woman has got better things to do than heal you. Like feed the seagulls and lead choirs formed by the voices in her head."

As she sank into the window seat vacated by Mister E, Val's knees nearly brushed the shoulder of the source of her petrified fingers, Sandra. The gorgon hunched over her mug on the floor, face hidden in her voluminous hood, her customary mirrored aviator sunglasses shielding her deadly eyes from turning anyone else's body parts to stone. Her hair-snakes moved beneath the fabric.

Val took a grateful sip of the coffee, closing her eyes and sighing as the taste of butterscotch cream hit her lips. She didn't blame Sandra for her stone fingers, though. The poor girl hadn't asked to become a gorgon. She needed compassion, not blame.

Turning her attention back to Malcolm's comment on Alice, she said, "From the cozy confines of our glass house, we do not have room to throw stones at Alice for being homeless. We're barely one step away from being out on the street ourselves." She eyed Malcolm over the rim of her mug and gestured at the scorched ceiling and boarded-up windows, the walls they were in the process of tearing down to the studs.

Their apartment had been firebombed by vampires, and had the creatures done a better job, they would all be sleeping out on the street. Fortunately, Val had used her magic to suck in enough fog and mist to put out the flames before the entire building burned down. Still, the front room of the flat was little more than a burned-out husk.

Rather than pay to have the damage fixed, they had convinced the landlord to let them do the repairs themselves in exchange for a couple of months' rent. It had seemed like an ingenious barter at the time.

Now, after hitting her thumb for the third time that day, Val was having second thoughts.

"Also, what the hell is up with your outfit?" Val asked. "Those overalls are at least four sizes too large. I can't decide if you're a train conductor or a hobo."

"Don't you know vertical stripes are slimming?" Malcolm grinned as he turned this way and that, modeling his overalls for her. He was shirtless beneath them, his lean frame a tent pole propping up the fabric. Combined with his blooming afro, he looked like a dandelion stalk ready to blow away. "I'll have you know that baggy overalls are the ultimate multi-purpose accessory. On the one hand, they're perfect for knocking out walls. On the other, if you wear the right clothing underneath them — or lack thereof — handsome strangers at the bar can slip their hands right inside your overalls and…"

"OK, I get the picture," Val interrupted. "I definitely do not need to hear the details of your sexcapades."

*"Aww, let the boy speak,"* Mister E complained. *"Just because you're a prude doesn't mean all of us are. I, for one, would welcome sexcapades in any form. Your sex life is as barren as Nevada in the summertime."*

"I like your overalls," Sandra said, her quiet voice emerging from the depths of her hood.

"Thank you. You see?" Malcolm turned and stuck his tongue out at Val.

Val scowled and handed Malcolm the hammer.

"Here, you knock down walls for a while. I've got to go to the bathroom."

"That's one thing I do not miss about being human," Malcolm observed. "So many bathroom breaks. Why didn't anyone ever tell me how efficient vampires' bodies are?"

Val squinted at him suspiciously. To save Hillary's life, Malcolm had recently become a vampire. He was handling the transition remarkably well. So well, in fact, that she suspected he was really just burying all his fears and putting on a happy face. Which meant the meltdown would probably be arriving later.

Well, there was nothing she could do about it. If Malcolm wanted to delude himself into thinking that being an undead bloodsucking parasite was some kind of improvement, she wasn't going to argue with him. She knew from personal experience that when you were a monster, you needed to grasp whatever self-delusion you could with both hands. Most days, it was the only thing that made her life even marginally livable.

Val left her creature-of-the-night roommate and headed down the hall. Fortunately, the rest of the apartment had only suffered smoke damage. She'd still needed to throw away her bedding and most of her clothing, but at least the structure was undamaged, and they'd been able to scrub most of the soot off the walls and ceiling.

Which was why Hillary was perched on top of a ladder in the middle of the hallway.

The pale vampire wore blue coveralls, her black hair tucked under a red bandana. The name patch on the coveralls read, "Butch." She was bent backward over the top of the ladder, scrubbing the ceiling over her head with a bucket of soapy water and a scrub brush.

"Doesn't that hurt?" Val asked. "My back is about to go out just looking at you."

Hillary chuckled as she straightened and moved a couple of steps down the ladder.

"Nope. Yet another benefit of being a vampire. Undead muscles don't cramp."

"Jeez, you and Malcolm make it sound so appealing."

"All the cool kids are doing it," Hillary grinned. "Your first taste is free."

"I bet it is. No, thank you. I enjoy having warm blood in my veins."

As Val reached for the bathroom door, Hillary was suddenly standing beside her. A startled squeak escaped her throat. The vampire smirked.

"I wanted to talk to you about something." Hillary leaned in close, her breath cool on Val's ear, her voice barely a whisper.

Val looked at her sideways, waiting for her housemate to continue.

"You know Malcolm's birthday is coming up."

"It is?"

Hillary rolled her eyes at Val. "Yes, it is. You really didn't know that? He's been dropping hints for the past month."

"I guess I didn't notice. I've been a bit distracted with"—she waved her fingers at the world—"everything."

"Understandable. But still. Malcolm hasn't been very subtle."

"Is Malcolm capable of being subtle?"

Hillary pursed her lips. "Now that you mention it, no, I don't think he is."

"Can you get to the point? I have to pee."

"I was thinking we could throw him a surprise party."

Val raised an eyebrow. "A surprise party? Where? In case you haven't noticed, our apartment is an active construction site."

"I thought maybe you could talk to Alain. He's got room."

"At the Mission Shifter's Settlement? I don't know if you've been there lately, but with all the new shifters that have been appearing, plus the new mayor's anti-shifter rhetoric, that place is like a refugee camp bursting at the seams. It's not exactly a festive atmosphere."

"Just ask Alain, OK? The worst that can happen is he'll say no. And in the meantime, you can start thinking of other places that might be big enough to host a party."

"Fine." Val sighed. "Can I pee now?"

"Sure, be my guest."

"A guest in my own bathroom. What an honor."

As Val was coming out of the bathroom a few minutes later, the front door burst open. She heard breathless voices. Striding down the hall, she found Rosa standing in the living room with a panicked look on her face.

Rosa looked terrible. She seemed to have lost twenty pounds, and bruised half-moons underlined her eyes. The Latina's skin was stretched so taut across her cheekbones and so pale, it looked like she hadn't seen the sun in months. Val could see the lines of her skull.

Rosa clutched at her arm. "Val, I had another dream. Something bad has happened."

"Slow down, Rosa. You've been having a lot of bad dreams lately. Why do you think this one is anything more than that?"

Rosa's eyes shimmered with tears.

"Because my nephew is missing."

# 3

Val sat Rosa down at the kitchen table and got her a cup of coffee. The woman's hands shook. Her clothes were so wrinkled, they looked like she'd slept in them, and they hung nearly as loose as Malcolm's overalls on her skeletal frame. She was a far cry from the confident, sassy shopkeeper who had been abducted by the fae Harbinger of Winter months ago.

"Tell me about the dream," Val said.

"It was raining and dark," Rosa replied. "I was looking down from the clouds, you know, looking down at the city lights, like I was flying. Bad things were happening below me. I couldn't see what, exactly, but knew they were. Bad people doing bad things, 'cause that's what they always do you know? I felt angry about it, but not like a hot anger. This anger was cold, like you get when you've thought about something so long it almost doesn't bother you anymore, but it's messed you up deep inside and now you're ready to crush somebody the same way you'd step on a cockroach. You know what I mean?"

Val didn't know. Her murderous rages were always burning hot, coming in the heat of the moment. But she wanted to keep Rosa moving forward, so she agreed. "Sure. And something bad is about to happen?"

Rosa nodded. "I'm drifting down out of the sky, the neighborhood coming into focus as I get closer to the ground. Then I see these gang-bangers roughing some guy up, and my view accelerates, like I'm a hawk, swooping down on them at full speed. Things move really fast after that, and there are screams and bones breaking and a lot of blood…" She trailed off, her haunted eyes no longer seeing the kitchen around her at all.

"And you think this wasn't a normal dream?"

Rosa shuddered. "No way. I've never had dreams like this before. They're too real."

"When did these dreams start?" Val asked.

"A couple of months ago. I'm not sure the exact date."

"After our run-in with the fae?"

"Yes. After that." Rosa looked up at Val, her eyes widening. "Do you think they're connected?"

"They could be. I don't know anything for certain, but it seems unlikely that you'd start having prophetic dreams after being abducted by the fae and they wouldn't be connected." Val sipped her coffee, eyebrows pinching above her nose. "Do you have proof that you're dreaming of actual events?"

"Yes. I dreamed about a house in flames in the lower Haight. I knew the house. A really nice old Victorian. I walked past it the next day to make sure it was still there. It was, no problem at all. Then a couple of days later it burned down. That was the first dream that came true. Or at least the first one I know about. There have been others since then."

"How many?"

"It's hard to say. The dreams were pretty sporadic at first. Lately, they've been happening almost every night. I can't sleep, I can't eat. And now my nephew is missing too. I don't know what to do, Val. I'm a nervous wreck. I can't keep going like this."

Val scowled into her mug, curling her fingers into a fist. Anger flushed her cheeks. Why was it always people she cared about?

"Did you see your nephew in the dream last night?"

"See him? No, I didn't see him. But I knew he was involved. You know that dream-intuition way when you're just sure of something?"

"Yeah, I get it." She sighed. "So, you want me to figure out where these dreams are coming from?"

Rosa looked at her like she was dim.

"No, I want you to find my nephew. I don't care where the dreams are coming from. Maybe they're my punishment for something I did. Maybe they're some kind of fucked-up blessing. Maybe the fae are sending them. It doesn't matter. I don't care about me. But when my family becomes involved, that matters. That shit matters a whole lot."

Val nodded. "OK. When was the last time you saw your nephew?"

She took notes as Rosa answered the usual checklist of who-what-when-where-why questions. When she had all the information she needed, she said, "I'll look into it. I'll let you know what I find out."

"Thank you," Rosa said. "And if you need money or something…"

"Money? Who said I needed money?"

"Well, I heard you were starting a supernatural detective agency, so I figured if I was going to ask for your help, I'd better be ready to pay."

"You heard? Who did you hear that from?"

"Oh, you know." Rosa twirled her fingers. "Word gets around."

"Word gets around, huh?" Val shot a glare in the direction of the living room, where she could see Malcolm swinging the sledge-hammer in his ridiculous overalls. "I wonder how that happens."

"No, it's a good thing," Rosa assured her. "We're all real happy you're doing it. There's too much weird shit happening in this city. It's nice to know there's somebody we can go to for help."

# 4

Like many western cities, San Francisco's Mission District was built on the backs of the Native American people. The district got its name from the Spanish mission erected on the banks of Mission Creek — which was definitely not its original name — around 1783. Thanks to the towering ridge of Twin Peaks deflecting the ever-present coastal winds and fog, the Mission District was generally sunnier and warmer than other parts of the chilly coastal peninsula.

As also happened in countless other parts of the Americas, the arrival of the Spanish spelled the end of thousands of years of peaceful habitation by the Native Americans. True to form, the invaders used steel and horses to impose their will, using the local Yelamu Indians, a branch of the Ohlone tribe, as slave labor to build their mission.

Since then, the Mission District had been occupied by generations of immigrants. In modern times, this had taken the form of many Mexicans and Latin Americans, who had been joined by sizable contingents of Asians and Pacific Islanders, including Chinese, Vietnamese and Filipinos forced out of Chinatown and other parts of the city by greedy developers.

Today, the Mission District was anything but sunny, however. Val kept the collar of her leather jacket turned up against the steady drizzle that had blanketed the city for weeks. As she strode past street vendors hawking everything from old buttons to live chickens to DIY genetic modification kits, she reflected on how the Collapse must have affected immigrant families. She couldn't imagine how devastating it would have been to suddenly find yourself cut off from your extended family, thousands of miles from home. Probably forever. From a global culture with the entire world in its reach, humanity had fallen back to a time of local isolationism in the blink of an eye. Of course, Val supposed that affected people who had families in Oklahoma or New Jersey too. As far as long-distance travel went, post-Collapse society had more in common with the 1800s than it did with the current century.

Val carried a low simmering anger with her as she thought about it. Anger for the native people who had been exploited and displaced. Anger for all those who had lost their families in the Collapse. And anger for those, like her, who had become monsters in the time since.

Beyond the physical and economic destruction, the Collapse had released a flood of magic into the world. And more monsters were popping up every day.

Val's hands curled into fists, fingernails slicing into her palms. She was angry a lot lately, and she didn't know why. The feeling was always there, like the buzz of a mosquito at the edge of her hearing. Setting her teeth on edge.

*"While you're walking, you should practice your weather sensing."* Mister E was a disembodied voice in her ear.

"Fine," Val snarled. She set her jaw and tried to concentrate.

The demon cat had been teaching her to expand her powers. First she'd worked on sensing the fluctuations in air pressure that heralded a change in the weather, which was where she started now. As she walked, Val stretched out her senses, feeling all the eddies and currents carried on the coastal winds. She sensed impending rain, which was hardly a revelation that required magical powers.

From there, she focused on pockets of denser air, where there was more moisture, finding a cloud that was fat and swollen. She used her dark mood to encourage this concentration, drawing in more moisture, making the cloud so heavy and black that it couldn't help but burst. A satisfied smirk curled her lip as her efforts provoked a sudden down-pour two blocks away.

Then she moved on to the really fun stuff. Lightning. She found a cloud crackling with unreleased electricity and channeled her seething discontent into it. Lightning flickered, and she focused harder, eventually forcing a small bolt to snake out and strike an adjacent cloud.

*"Not bad. You're still too slow, though. You should be able to provoke lightning in an instant."*

"Slavedriver." Despite the cat's words, she grinned at her achievement. Creating lightning bolts was pretty spectacular, no matter how long it took to make them.

Her destination finally came into view: a tiny herb shop tucked into an alley off 19th. Rosa had told her this shop had some connection to Jorge's disappearance, but she wasn't sure what. All Rosa had was a feeling she'd gotten from one of her dreams.

Val shrugged as she stopped in front of the little storefront. She'd spent time chasing worse leads.

The front window of the herb shop was so dirty she could barely see inside from the sidewalk out front. A bell tinkled as she pushed the door open and stepped through.

Inside, the tiny space was just as dingy as the front window had promised. Colorful bowls full of ground herbs weighed down sagging shelves, and burlap sacks stuffed with dried roots slouched in the corners. The narrow aisles were barely passable, and things clutched at her leather jacket as she worked her way deeper into the cluttered store. There was no sign of any other people.

Finally, she discovered a counter, which seemed just as deserted as the rest of the store. She reached out and tapped a brass bell with a faded sign reading, "Ring for service."

The chime of the bell was weirdly muffled, the sound swallowed by the thick, dusty air. As the echoes died out, a heavy silence resettled over the shop.

Val waited.

No response.

Annoyed, she rang the bell again.

A flurry of movement burst from behind a pegboard wall hung

with dried stalks, and a weathered voice cried out, "One minute, one minute. Don't be in such a hurry. Patience is the mother of success."

A tiny Vietnamese woman came bustling out, wrapped in a proliferation of shawls and scarves. She seemed to be mostly made up of wrinkles, squinting up at Val from under a loose bun of shining silver hair.

The woman bared her teeth, revealing a smile full of gaps. "What are you looking for?"

"Funny you should phrase it like that," Val said. "When's the last time you saw Jorge Alvares?"

The woman's smile pinched into a scowl.

"That bum. He's supposed to be writing a contract for me. He did not show up for our appointment last week."

"Did you try to contact him?"

"Sure. I text his phone, but he never respond." The woman made a spitting motion before repeating, "That bum."

"Do you know where he lives?"

"He is out near the hospital." The little woman pointed south.

"Do you have an address?"

The old woman stopped and squinted up at Val.

"You a cop?"

"No, I'm a … I'm working for his family. He's disappeared and they're worried about him. Any information you have could be very valuable."

The woman's eyes lit up at the word.

"Valuable, eh? Maybe I know where he lives. How much that information worth to you?"

Val sighed.

"That was a poor choice of words. I don't really have any loose funds at the moment."

The woman's expression closed like a door.

"This is a business. Stop wasting my time. You go now."

Without another word, the woman spun and bustled into the back of the shop.

"If I could just…" Val called after her, but it was no use. The old woman was gone.

"*That was smoothly done,*" Mister E snarked. "*I think your friends are right. You really should do this detective stuff professionally.*"

"Eat socks," Val retorted.

She grimaced as her eyes searched the interior of the shop again. Jorge had lived out by the hospital. That narrowed it down some, at least. Of course there were probably thousands of Alvares's who lived out by the hospital. Finding his apartment was not going to be easy.

Movement caught her eye. Something flashing along one of the shelves. A small furred body disappearing behind a basket of dried ginger root.

Val made a face. "Looks like there are rats in here, too. Lovely."

"*That was no rat,*" Mister E was suddenly alert, his gray fur standing on end. "*Look closer. Use my eyes.*"

Val did as he asked, overlaying the demon cats' vision over her own. Instantly, the shop was filled with eddies of orange and gold power, drifting through the dusty air like fog. Several bowls of herbs glowed, and whatever was in a closed burlap sack in the corner shone so brightly it almost blinded her.

"Why didn't you tell me this place was full of magic?"

"*You didn't ask,*" Mister E said smugly. "*Besides, the entire city is full of magic. We'd never get anywhere if I interrupted you every time we came across something magical.*"

"When I'm on an investigation and I walk into a magical herb shop, I'd appreciate a heads up."

"*I can't make any promises. I've got a lot on my plate.*" The cat sat down and began to lick his back leg.

Val ground her teeth against the urge to throttle him as she turned her attention back to the shelf where she'd seen the creature. There was nothing visible now. She cautiously poked her head behind a bowl of red powder. At the far end of the shelf, hidden in the shadows, a pair of bright eyes looked back at her. The small creature's body exuded magic like a hot stone giving off heat.

"There you are," Val breathed. "What are you?"

The creature didn't move. It just sat there, staring back at her, nose twitching.

"Can you understand me? You can come out, I won't hurt you."

Slowly, the creature hopped forward, until Val could make out the outline of its fluffy body. Above the active nose and bright eyes, long ears twitched at every sound.

"A rabbit," Val breathed. "That's it. Come on out. It's all right."

The rabbit moved into the light, its pale fur shining like the full moon. It hopped toward the door, then turned and looked back at her, eyes glowing.

"Are you coming or not?" The rabbit's voice was the incongruent rasp of a Brooklyn truck driver.

Val stifled a surprised laugh.

"You can talk?"

"No." The words resonated in her mind. "It's all in your head."

The rabbit turned tail and was gone.

# 5

Val tracked the rabbit into the alley outside. It sat upright, nose twitching, as if waiting to be sure she'd seen it. When she had, the rabbit hopped away. It paused at the next intersection and looked back again.

"Why do you think it wants me to follow it?" Val asked.

*"Perhaps it wants to take you to Mr. McGregor's carrot patch. Why you believe any good can come of chasing rabbits through alleys is beyond me."* Mister E bared his teeth in a wicked grin. *"Unless you plan on killing and eating it. Then I'm one hundred percent on board."*

"Gross. Nobody eats rabbits anymore."

*"You are mistaken. And rabbits are delicious. Did you look in the cages of the street vendors we passed on the way here? I saw at least three selling rabbits. Not to mention cages full of pigeons, dogs, and rats. I even saw a cage full of cats. Barbarians."* He shuddered.

"You do remember you're not really a cat, don't you?"

He unleashed his Cheshire grin. *"I like to stay in character. But you're right, I don't actually care all that much. If people want to eat cats, that's their business. Though cat meat is stringy and not particularly flavorful, so I still have to object on the grounds of personal standards. People shouldn't eat cats because they simply don't taste good."*

"Wait, are you saying the dogs we saw are for eating?" Val looked horrified.

Mister E's grin grew, the corners stretching out past the edges of his face.

*"Without a doubt. Dogs are delicious. Especially those little round ones. They're like fatty sausages."*

Val grimaced and dropped the subject.

The rabbit proved the old woman hadn't been lying, leading them generally south, in the direction of the hospital. The creature proved adept at keeping itself hidden, dashing between places of concealment in brief flashes of white. Nobody else noticed its presence.

"What do you think the deal is with the rabbit?" Val asked.

*"I believe it's a Moon Rabbit."*

"A what?"

*"A minor magical creature from East Asian mythologies. The Moon Rabbit assists the Moon Goddess in making alchemical compounds and is often depicted pounding away with a mortar and pestle. Some claim the rabbit is making an elixir of immortality."*

"The Moon Goddess? You're not telling me the old woman in that shop was a Moon Goddess, are you?"

*"Well … I'm not 'not' telling you that."*

"Great. Now there are goddesses running around the city." Val sighed. "I thought vampires were bad enough."

*"There have always been gods and goddesses in the city. Historically speaking, immigrants have always brought their gods with them. Don't worry, a goddess' strength depends on her followers, and even in a city as international as this one, I doubt that particular Moon Goddess has many followers left. Her powers are probably negligible. In practice, she is more or less what she seems: an old woman running an herb shop."*

"I'm not sure if that's reassuring or depressing."

*"Well, at least she's still alive. When gods are forgotten by all their follow-ers, they fade into oblivion. So someone still remembers her."*

Ahead, Val heard voices. Angry voices, chanting and shouting. The rain thickened as she came out of an alley and found herself on the edge of a throng of people holding signs. She narrowed her eyes, wondering what they were worked up about this week. In the post-

Collapse economy, things were always running out, and people were forever getting worked up about it.

"You'd think they'd have learned to be more flexible by now," she muttered. "When there's a shortage, you've got to roll with it. Marching and shouting isn't going to change anything. It's not like Mayor Light has the power to magically end the shortages. If he even gives a shit. Which I doubt."

*"Val,"* Mister E said tersely. *"That's not what's happening here."*

She followed his gaze and noticed that the crowd wasn't marching down the street and yelling to the uncaring gods the way they usually did. They seemed to be gathering around a single point. Their anger had a focus.

The crowd parted for a moment and Val saw what they were circling around. Or rather, who.

A young girl stood with tears streaming down her face, her hands held defensively over her head. She was half-shifted — her ears long and furred, jaw slightly elongated and covered in fine red fur. A fox shifter. Even half-shifted, Val could tell the girl's human features had an Asian cast to them. Was she a kitsune like Obi in Japantown?

The crowd surrounded the girl. Rough hands shoving her. People spitting on her.

Val finally noticed the signs the people were carrying. Freaks out of Frisco. Monster Free Mission. In Mayor Light We Trust.

"They're going to tear that girl apart," she said. "Hey! Stop!"

She pushed her way into the crowd, shouldering people aside as she fought to reach the shifter girl.

A big man's hand grabbed her shoulder.

"Take it easy there, little lady."

She pivoted and drove her elbow into the man's midsection. His breath exploded out of him as he folded like a paper bag.

"I have somewhere to go," she snapped.

She turned to continue on her course, only to find another man had stepped in front of her. He had broad shoulders and blond hair shorn close to the scalp. A cheap tattoo climbed the side of his neck. Two more men came from the sides, boxing her in.

"You really don't want to do this," she told them, narrowing her eyes as she reached for her magic.

The man blocking her way leered at her, his silver teeth glinting. "Oh, but we really do."

A hand grabbed her ass, and then everything happened at once.

Val dropped onto one knee and whipped a fist back into the grabby guy's crotch. He squeaked with pain and she whirled, preparing to send a gust of wind at the men flanking her.

As she brought up her hands to blast them, a great weight slammed onto her shoulders, smashing her down and grinding her cheek against the gravel. She squirmed and cursed, but she was pinned by the man's weight, with no leverage and no room to strike back.

"You're a feisty one." The man flipped her over like a beached fish, keeping her pinned with his knees. Silver teeth flashed as he grinned. "I like my girls feisty."

Val grinned right back at him, her anger blazing like a furnace.

"You have no idea how feisty I am. I've even got a new trick for you."

She closed her eyes and found the storm. Focused on the pressure and electricity in the air. Gathering it, nurturing it, building it until her skin tingled. The metal in the man's teeth called to the electricity. A human lightning rod.

The bolt that lanced down was so bright the entire world turned white, even through her closed lids. The sound was like a cannon blast. She heard the man's shriek of pain and surprise, felt him convulse as electricity surged through his body. It branched out from there, drawn to the others in the crowd nearby, the water in their bodies, convulsing half a dozen people.

Val yelped as a bit of the current ran through her as well, making her legs kick and her hands tingle. She'd have to be more careful of spillover in the future.

Still, her lips peeled back in a feral grin. She'd called down the lightning when she needed it!

On the heels of her strike, the air pressure plummeted. The rain intensified, becoming a true downpour, falling so heavily she could feel the weight pushing her down.

There was something else in the air too. Something she couldn't quite put her finger on. A force, dark and powerful.

Through the roar of the pounding rain and the high-pitched ringing in her ears, Val heard other sounds. Voices raised in fear and anger. People screaming.

The rain coated her face, running into her eyes, her nose, her mouth, filling her throat. She struggled to breathe.

Three steps away, the shifter girl, a thick sheen of water coating her face like paint, clawed at her throat. Val lunged and wrapped her arms around the girl. She reached for her power, fighting to push the water away from the two of them, to create a tiny bubble of space in the deluge. Slowly, the water was forced away from their faces. The girl gasped and sobbed as her breath returned.

Sucking in air herself, Val tried to see what was happening, but the world beyond the rain was no more than an impressionistic watery smear. Vague shapes moving. People spinning in panic and desperation, arms outstretched, eyes wide with fear.

A dark shape moved among them. Gliding tall and silent through the rain. Wherever this shape passed, people fell.

When Val's vision finally cleared, she was surrounded by bodies scattered on the pavement. Twisted and broken, washed ashore like branches in the flood.

As she struggled to her feet, she finally got a look at the newcomer. The rain seemed heavier around the dark figure, blurring his outline. All she could make out was a tall frame draped in a long trench coat.

She gathered her magic, preparing to defend herself, but the figure didn't attack her. He simply turned a dark gaze in her direction, silent beneath the curtain of water.

She cast her eyes around the street, at the twisted bodies of the protestors. Their faces were grotesque — swollen and puffy, as if they'd drowned on dry land. Her stomach lurched and she tasted bile.

"You killed them all. You almost killed me. Who are you?"

The figure cocked his head at her. She couldn't make out his features, but a deep sense of sadness emanated from him. He raised his hand and the rain intensified around her, water pushing down over her face once again.

Val gritted her teeth and pushed back, using her power to bend the water away. She grunted and cursed, her anger rising as she stubbornly fought for breath. The downpour was so heavy it felt like she was trying to lift a bear. But she would not give in.

The wail of an approaching siren made the figure's head whip around. Following his dark gaze, Val saw blue and red lights flashing. Getting closer.

Lighting flashed, natural this time, and the world became a faded red afterimage. The pressure of the water against her face lessened until it was only a light rain once more.

By the time the echoes of the thunder had finally died away, the dark figure was gone.

# 6

"What was that?" Val breathed as she surveyed the alley. No one moved. The wail of the approaching siren was getting louder.

*"I don't know, but whatever it was, he solved your little crowd problem."* Mister E appeared, blowing smoke rings with his candy cigarette. *"You should probably thank him the next time you see him."*

"Thank him? He just killed dozens of people. If I hadn't been able to bend the water away from our faces, he would have drowned me and the shifter girl too." She knelt next to the man with the silver teeth, pressing her fingertips to his neck, just to be sure. His skin was cold. No pulse. "You want me to thank him for that?"

*"Don't be a hypocrite, Val. You've killed plenty of people yourself."*

"On accident. The only things I kill on purpose are monsters. That man — or whatever he was — just murdered these people in cold blood."

*"The word you're searching for is bigots. They were dirty bigots who were probably going to kill that shifter girl. If they had succeeded, are you telling me you wouldn't have killed them yourself?"*

"But they didn't kill her. And they wouldn't have. I had the situation under control."

Mister E laughed. *"Pinned on your back in the gravel. Yes, you definitely had it under control."*

"The girl! She was right here. Where did she go?" Val's eyes widened and she spun, examining the bodies. Every single one of the corpses was pale and bloated. "How do you drown on dry land?"

She turned bodies over one after another, scanning faces. Finally, she found the girl lying beside the swollen body of a dead black woman. She was unconscious, and her features had reverted to human. She looked maybe sixteen.

Val knelt and placed her fingers against the girl's neck. After a long moment she felt a pulse and breathed a sigh of relief.

"She's still alive. And the police are almost here. They'll take care of her." She gently smoothed the girl's hair, then swiveled her head, surveying the carnage. "There's nothing else I can do for her. Where do you suppose the Moon Rabbit went?"

*"Maybe the mob scared it away."*

"Or maybe that rain-man did." She peered behind dumpsters and into shadowy nooks. No rabbit.

*"Either way, it looks like the thing has run off."*

"Great. So this whole trip was a waste of time."

*"Not a complete waste of time. It looks like you'll have a chance to catch up with your friends in the SFPD."*

Right on cue, the squad car screeched to a halt at the edge of the crowd, blue and red lights flashing.

Val sighed. "Great, just the way I was hoping to spend my day."

The passenger door of the car popped open and a familiar figure stepped out. Detective Chen paid no heed to the rain, the drops running off his close-cropped black hair. He was as weathered as old driftwood, his hair fading to silver at the temples, deep lines gathered at the corners of his eyes. A younger woman trailed behind him, charcoal skin over a well-pressed pant suit, her hair sculpted into a crest. She eyed Val suspiciously from beneath her black umbrella but said nothing, letting Chen take the lead.

Detective Chen's eyes had bags under them, but his gaze was sharp as he took in the scene at a glance. His lips pressed into a line as he strode toward Val, flipping open an old school notepad and pulling a silver pen from his shirt pocket.

"Val Keri at a murder scene. Imagine my surprise," he said flatly.

"I didn't kill anyone, Detective."

"Of course not. You are the most conveniently murder-adjacent person I've ever met in my life." He bent to get a closer look at the body of the man with the silver teeth. "So are you going to tell me what happened, here, Keri? Why is my street full of bodies?"

Val grimaced.

"I'm afraid I don't have much of an answer for you. I was passing through when I found this mob harassing this shifter girl. I tried to intervene and they assaulted me. I was fighting them off when a man shrouded in rain appeared."

"Shrouded in rain?" the woman trailing Chen asked. "What does that even mean?"

"I'm sorry, do I know you?" Val asked.

Chen performed the introductions.

"Val Keri, this is my new partner, Latisha James."

Latisha crossed her arms over her chest, her gaze suspicious.

"Shrouded in rain?" she prompted.

"It means he was a dark shape behind a curtain of rain. He looked like he was hiding behind the water."

"How is that possible?"

"I have no idea. I've never seen anything like it before."

Latisha scowled and Chen made a few notes. The fact that he didn't challenge Val's story was a testament to just how many strange situations they had encountered together.

Out of the corner of her eye, Val saw movement. The shifter girl was sitting up and moving. Beside her sat the white rabbit, soft nose pressed into the girl's palm.

"That girl is still alive, by the way. She could use medical attention."

"The ambulance is already on its way," Chen said. "What happened after that?"

"I don't really know. The rain got so thick I could hardly see my own hands. It was all I could do to keep it away from my face so I could breathe. When it cleared up, this is what I saw." She waved her hands at the corpses.

Latisha snorted. "That is the biggest load of BS I've ever heard. Dozens of people dead, and you say you didn't see what happened because of the rain? You expect us to believe that?"

"I don't give a shit what you believe," Val snapped. "That's what happened."

Latisha got in Val's face. "How about we take you down to the station and see if you change your story?"

"I'd like to see you try."

"Everyone calm down," Chen snapped. "Detective James, we're not taking Ms. Keri down to the station."

"Why not? She's obstructing our investigation with her bullshit rain story. And, in case you haven't noticed, she's standing in a street full of dead bodies. The only survivors seem to be her and a shifter girl?" James's face screwed up in disgust as she gestured toward the unconscious girl. "That alone is plenty of reason to take her in."

"Seriously?" Val snorted. "Where'd you get this one, Chen? Straight out of the Police Academy?"

"That's it," Latisha pulled out her handcuffs. "Turn around. Hands against the wall."

"Detective James, stand down." Chen's voice cracked like a whip, making both Val and Latisha jump. He glared at them, his expression hard. "Ms. Keri is not a suspect here. I know the circumstances look suspicious, but I'm the senior officer and you're going to have to trust me on this."

"Just like that?" His partner gaped at him. When Chen didn't waver, she threw up her hands. "If we're not going to question her, then what are we even doing here?"

"I never said we weren't going to question her. She's a witness. Of course we're going to question her. What I said was that we're not taking her into custody. Now, you're going to stand down and let me take the lead. Are we clear?"

Latisha rolled her eyes and folded her arms over her chest. "Yes, sir."

The younger detective stood and glared while Chen took Val's statement. The ambulance arrived as she was finishing up, and they watched the EMTs take the girl away.

"Shifters." Chen sighed and glanced at Val. "You know, this job was a lot easier when all this monsters and magic shit was imaginary. The first time I met you, I thought you were just another flaky Wiccan. Now we've got shifters living out in the open, Mayor Light actively campaigning against them, and dozens of bodies in the street. I've seen people transformed into indescribable horrors. Gutted like fish. Things I wish I could unsee."

Val scowled at the Bosch painting surrounding them.

"You and me both, Detective. Can I go now?"

"Yes, you can go."

As she walked away, Latisha James called out to her retreating back, "I'm watching you, Keri."

"Yeah," Val shot back. "Right now, you're watching my ass."

# 7

"*What now?*" Mister E floated on his back beside Val, blowing candy smoke rings up at the sky. The light rain falling passed right through his incorporeal form.

Val frowned. "The Moon Rabbit stayed back there with that shifter-girl. So I guess now we use some good old fashioned detective skills."

"*Do you have any of those?*"

"Very funny."

"*I'm just saying. Throwing magic at a problem isn't the same thing as an actual professional investigation.*"

"Watch and learn, furball."

She crossed Caesar Chavez Street and walked until she was near the area where, according to the Moon Goddess, Rosa's nephew lived. Then she started asking questions.

"Excuse me, have you seen this man?" Val flashed the picture Rosa had given her.

Most of the people she approached ignored her or brushed her off, but after about an hour she finally encountered a bent-backed old Mexican woman wheeling a cart full of groceries home from the local bodega. The woman peered suspiciously from beneath her shawl.

"Are you a cop?"

"No, I'm a friend. His family is worried about him. They haven't heard from him in weeks."

At the word family, the suspicion cleared from the woman's gaze.

"Oh, that's terrible. Family is the most important thing." Even though there was no one else on the sidewalk, she leaned close to Val as if someone might be listening. "Of course I know Jorge. He lives in my building. Nice boy, but a little quiet. Come, I'll show you."

Her suspicions erased, the woman chattered away as Val followed her back to a tired apartment building. Weathered shadows marred the once bright yellow exterior paint, the entire building leaning drunkenly against its neighbor. The old woman ignored all this as she opened the front door and ushered Val into the entranceway. She inhaled the scents of worn wood, pine cleaner, and fried onions. The woman pointed to an exhausted line of brass mailboxes sagging along the wall.

"That's his mailbox. I think it's full, the mail has been stacking up on top."

Val leafed through the accumulated letters but found only the usual assortment of junk mail. For a moment she marveled that, of all things, junk mail was somehow still going strong after the Collapse.

"Junk mail and cockroaches," she muttered. "Civilization may be long gone, but junk mail and cockroaches will always survive."

*"And Twinkies,"* Mister E added.

"And Twinkies," she agreed, noting the number on the mailbox: 5D.

"I can walk you up to his door, if you like," the old woman said.

"No, I can take it from here. Thank you for your help." Val gave the woman a friendly wave and headed up the stairs.

Apartment 5D ended up being on the third floor at the back of the building, just beyond a strip of worn gray carpet that might have been green at some point in the past. The door was locked, but after a few determined minutes with a set of lock picks, Val pushed it open and stepped inside.

The stale air smelled of rot, and a peek inside the trash can unearthed a putrid mound of mold and maggots that made Val wish she hadn't looked. Her stomach tried to climb up her throat and she opened a protesting window to hang her head outside, gulping in the rain-washed air. The building next door was so close her head almost brushed the wall.

Her stomach finally settled and she got to work, searching the apartment for anything that might tell her where Jorge had gone. An unmade bed stood in the corner of the small studio, but the blanket and pillow on the sagging couch attested that he habitually slept there. A cello sulked in the corner, while a dusty pile of video game cartridges told Val that before the Collapse he might have been the type of guy to watch TV or play video games. But the city grid didn't support that much electricity use anymore, so it looked like he now read a lot of comics and old magazines instead. She leafed through the pile and found that he preferred horror comics and manga to super-heroes, but his choice of reading materials didn't really tell her much about him, or give her any hints as to where he had disappeared to. Or why.

She leafed through his clothes rack, noting the fine weave of his suit jackets against her fingertips. He favored bright silk ties. Polished black shoes stood ready for action beneath the rack. This jived with what Rosa had told her about Jorge's law practice. Rosa thought her nephew even did some work for Mayor Light.

In the bathroom, Val found a comb with black hairs wedged between the teeth. She plucked out a few and filled her pocket with the hair before pushing the kitchen table and chairs aside to make space on the floor. Val drew a careful pentagram with a piece of chalk, placing candle stubs at the corners.

*"Good old-fashioned detective skills, eh?"* Mister E snarked.

"I think magic is about as old-fashioned as you can get, don't you?" Val replied smoothly. "Mages have been around a lot longer than detectives."

The demon-cat chuckled. *"You may have missed your true calling as a lawyer."*

"Law. Magic. Either way, it's all about the loopholes."

She settled herself inside the pentagram and chanted a quick tracking spell, then burned one of the hairs. She watched the smoke closely to see in which direction it would drift. It drifted toward the ceiling and then ... it just kind of sat there, swirling about aimlessly.

Val scowled. "That's not helpful."

*"Maybe he moved upstairs."*

"No, the smoke isn't indicating up as a direction. It's just rising the way smoke does naturally. It's not actually giving me anything."

*"Perhaps he's dead."*

"Even if he was dead, the smoke should still drift in the direction of his body. I don't know what's wrong with it."

She watched the smoke for another minute. It refused to do anything of interest.

*"So, now what?"*

Val sighed and held up a small flier she'd found sitting on an end table.

"Now I guess I have to go back to those old-fashioned detective skills."

# 8

The Imaginarium had changed since Val's last visit. Which was not surprising. The collective workspace occupied an abandoned paper factory, and it was always evolving as people put up or took down various sculptures and decorations, or moved the walls of their cubicles. The old brick building had a metal roof like an airplane hanger's, with massive, curving rib support beams. A life-sized blue whale sculpture flew high above everyone, suspended from the ribs, aluminum tail waving lazily up and down. Sprawling banks of single-pane windows set high in the walls grudgingly allowed dusty daylight in. The entire space smelled of sawdust, rust, nutmeg and coffee.

The open manufacturing floor had been repurposed and partitioned into dozens of workshops. Craftspeople and artists occupied the spaces: sculptors, ceramicists, welders, tailors, brewers and blacksmiths. The list went on. The roof arched high above the eight-foot partition walls, and the sounds of their work echoed around the space, filling Val's ears with a pleasant cacophony as she stepped through the double iron doors of the main entrance and headed for the one person she knew in the collective workspace.

Gunter Gristle was bent over his workbench when Val stuck her head into his cubicle. The tip of his pointed ears poked through his shaggy hair, and the troll's bushy eyebrows were a wild tangle around the dark goggles resting on his forehead. The coarse hair covering the greenish skin on his arms and hands was so thick it could probably be called fur, and he wore no shoes on his massive, thickly callused feet. He was pounding out dents with a hammer so big it would look right at home in the hands of Thor.

Val had commissioned Gunter to fashion a pair of custom hand-cuffs when she had hunted the Puca. The cuffs had tightened and loosened along with the meddlesome shapeshifter so the Puca couldn't wriggle out of them. In payment, the troll had requested and received an odd bounty of wine, rat meat, and comic books.

Gunter was so intent on his work that it took him almost a full minute to notice Val in the doorway, watching him. When he did, he yelped and staggered back, nearly dropping the big hammer on his clawed toes.

"By all the gods, don't sneak up on me like that!" he rumbled. "You'll give me a heart attack."

Val snorted.

"Standing in your doorway is hardly sneaking. It's not my fault you're so wrapped up in your work that you don't pay attention to your surroundings."

The troll peered down at her, his face splitting into a wide smile. "Val Keri, what brings you here? Do you have more comic books for me?"

"That depends on if you can help me or not." Val held up Jorge's picture. "Have you seen this man?"

Gunter grabbed a pair of round glasses off a shelf and slid them onto his bulbous nose. The glasses had several lenses on little arms, which opened up like a sunburst. He clicked two of the lenses into place and squinted at the picture. After a moment, he shook his head.

"Nope, sorry. I can't say that I have. Why did you think I would?"

"I found this in his apartment." Val handed over a postcard flyer. It advertised music lessons at the Imaginarium.

"Oh, that." Gunter waved his thick hand dismissively. "That's nothing to do with me. I'm tone deaf as a sea lion."

"Do you know whose flyer this is?"

The troll made a face. "It belongs to that pixie over on the east side. Calls herself Feather. Annoying little thing, always zipping about and gossiping."

"Where can I find her?"

"Under the crystal waterfall."

"Crystal waterfall?"

Gunter pointed above the cubicles with one gnarled finger. Val followed it and found, sure enough, a crystal waterfall cascading from the arching ceiling. It sparkled and shifted in the light, creating the illusion that it was flowing downward.

"The pixie's studio is right below the falls. You can't miss it."

"Thanks, Gunter. I owe you one." Val slid the flyer and picture back into her jacket pocket and turned to go.

"You owe me two comics," he called after her. "I like mutants!"

Val waved in acknowledgement.

Knowing where you were going and getting there in the Imaginarium meant two very different things. There was no floor plan. People simply found an open section of floor and erected walls or shelves, or whatever, to claim it as their workspace. The entire place was a maze of twisting passages that sometimes abruptly became dead ends. Although she could see the sparkling waterfall clearly as she walked, actually getting to it took Val nearly half an hour.

Making her way through the Imaginarium, she examined art installations and peered into doorways. The variety of the workspaces was staggering. She saw a sewing studio, a welding shop, leatherworkers, paper cutters, rock polishers, painters, musicians, a small theater troupe, a bakery, a Tai Chi dojo, and even a ceramicist's kiln. The interior of the spacious old factory was like a small city, with artisans and craftspeople of every discipline she could think of, and quite a few that she wasn't aware of until she peered into the open doors of their workshops. Who had ever heard of anyone making vests from fish scales?

Eventually, she found herself standing in front of a cork bulletin board. Overlapping notices clamored for her attention. Classes in art, music, and baking. Potlucks and community game nights. Political posters.

Of this last variety, one in particular drew her eye. Val frowned as she bent to get a better look at it.

*Freaks out of Frisco.*

*San Francisco for San Franciscans.*

"Looks like Mayor Light's propaganda is everywhere." She sighed.

Charles Light had swept into power with a campaign of fear. He specialized in rabble-rousing speeches, and his campaign slogan, San Francisco for San Franciscans, drew clear lines around the people who were and were not welcome in his city.

In a world of post-Collapse scarcity, it was easy to prey on people's fears of losing what little they had. After all, most people had already lost everything once. Though they did their best to go about their lives, in the back of their minds was the constant fear that they could lose it all again.

Playing on that fear was the cheapest kind of political theater. Unfortunately, it was also extremely effective. People were desperate for safety and security. Charles Light promised them that. All they had to do was turn their fear into anger, and use that anger against everyone who didn't fit Light's narrow definition of 'San Franciscan.'

The most frequent target of his fire-and-brimstone speeches was the newly emerging supernatural community, and shifters were the most visible and easiest marks. Mayor Light blamed the shifters for just about everything that was wrong with the city, and violent attacks against shifters, such as the mob scene Val had stumbled upon earlier, were becoming more and more common.

"I worry about my friends," she said.

*"As you should,"* Mister E replied. For once his voice contained no sarcasm. Now it was the cold voice of a killer. *"People who rely on mass hysteria to do their dirty work are the worst kind of scum. And the hardest to fight. At heart, people are little more than herd animals; they find it easiest to simply go along with the crowd. Especially when that crowd is fueled by emotion. They let themselves get swept up by the passion of others and their brains turn off. I've seen it countless times."*

"I have too," Val whispered.

A memory of the village she'd grown up in came to her unbidden.

Children yelling and chasing her. Surrounding her. Pelting her with sharp rocks and sharper words.

Her heart leapt frantically against her ribs. Her breath came in gasps. Sweat broke out across her forehead.

Val swallowed hard and ground her fingernails into her palms, fighting to get her panic under control. That had been a long time ago. Decades. That village was on another continent entirely. Those children were far, far away. None of them could threaten her now.

With the advantage of time and perspective, she could see that they hadn't been bad children, not really. They were just caught up in the moment. In the emotion. Playing a teasing game that had snowballed and gotten out of control. Gone too far and gotten ugly.

That was the moment she'd first met Mister E. Surrounded by taunting children on a rocky mountaintop. She could still smell the scent of honey that filled her nostrils as his voice whispered in her mind, *"I can give you the power to fight back. All you have to do is free me."*

Tormented and pelted with rocks. Tears and snot running down her face. What child wouldn't agree in that moment?

Val had accepted the demon-cat's bargain.

And he had kept his word, filling her with the power to fight back.

And fight back she had. She had summoned the winds for the first time, hurling dirt and debris back at her tormentors. Wanting to return the hurt to those who were hurting her. All her anger, fear, and frustration exploding out of her in a desperate wave.

Many of the children had been badly hurt.

Some had died.

Her best friend, Katrina, and her own mother were among the casualties.

Val's fingers strayed to her shoulder — to the memento mori tattoo hidden beneath her jacket, the inked memorial to Katrina and her mother. And all the others whose deaths she carried on her conscience.

She had done many bad things in her life. She had lost control of her power and people had died. She could never wipe the dark stains from her soul.

This was why she fought the darkness. Tried to help others. She was doing her best to balance the scales.

Even if, deep down, she knew it was an impossible task. Her guilt was too heavy. There was no hope of balancing the things she'd done.

Val shook herself and turned away from the bulletin board. It was time to get back to work. She had a friend who needed her help.

# 9

Val emerged from the maze of corridors and found herself in a space that looked more like an indoor meditation center than a workshop. Ivy-draped branches formed living walls around a plot of rich soil. She couldn't tell if the soil had been laid on top of the floor or if the cement had been torn up to reveal the soil beneath. Round river stones lined paths that wound through a fragrant garden, opening into a peaceful glade in the center. Here she found a large circle with cushion-covered stones, stumps, and small trees whose branches had been woven together to form natural chairs.

A small woman bent over a spray of honeysuckle to one side of the circle. She was perhaps the most petite woman Val had ever seen, barely four feet tall and slight as a willow branch.

"Excuse me," Val said.

The woman looked up at her with a radiant smile.

"Oh, come in, come in!" Before Val knew what was happening, the woman had flitted over, taken her by the elbow, and was pulling her into the circle. "Sit down, sit down!"

"I, uh…" Val tried to extract her elbow, but the tiny woman had a surprisingly strong grip. In desperation, she pulled out Jorge's picture. "Have you seen…"

"All in good time. Sit, sit." The woman waved the picture away without looking at it and pushed Val into one of the woven branch chairs. "What kind of tea would you like?"

"Tea?"

"I have mint, chamomile, pennyroyal, oolong, earl grey, lapsang souchong…"

"Do you have coffee?" Val cut in.

The little woman's lips pinched in disapproval.

"Coffee is for barbarians."

"I guess you can call me Conan then."

"Tea is all I serve."

"I don't really need anything. If I could just ask…" Again, Val tried to show her the picture.

Again, the woman overrode her.

"Things must be done in the proper order. Tea first. If you don't know what kind you want, I can pick something for you."

Val sighed. Clearly she wasn't going to get anywhere without the tea ceremony.

"That would be fine."

Five minutes later, Val cupped a steaming mug as big as a bowl in both hands. She suspected that it was, in fact, a bowl, but she kept the thought to herself. The rich brew inside the mug/bowl was almost as dark as coffee, and sweet cream swirled inside it like a galaxy unfurling. She had to admit it smelled good, and when — at Feather's insistence — she took a cautious sip, she found the flavor rich and dark. Almost nutty beneath the sweet layer of cream. Not at all the way she expected tea to taste.

At Val's expression, Feather nodded.

"There. You do like tea. You just haven't had the right tea before." She took a sip of her own mug — a dainty thing with a curling china handle — and smiled.

"I suppose I do," Val admitted. "What kind of tea is it?"

"Dandelion root. Now, what can I do for you?"

"I'm looking for this man." Val again held out the photograph.

Feather beamed. "Jorge! Such a sweet man. He's been learning to play the cello."

"When was the last time you saw him?"

The little woman tapped a finger against her lips. "Let's see, he usually comes to class on Tuesdays, but I think he missed last week, so I suppose it must have been the week before that. Why?"

"He's missing and his family is worried about him. Do you know what he liked to do? Anywhere he might have hung out after class?"

"Oh, I wouldn't know. I maintain a proper professional distance. But some of his classmates might. Why don't you come back this evening and ask them?"

With a start, Val realized that today was, in fact, Tuesday.

"Uh, sure. What time?"

"The class starts at seven."

"OK. I'll do that."

---

Feather's dandelion root tea had only whetted Val's appetite for the real thing. So, with some time to kill before the pixie's music class, she knew just where to go.

Zombie Coffee had finally reopened following the damage caused by a woman turning into a gorgon inside the shop. That woman, of course, was Sandra, Val's former housemate who now lived in an apartment in the basement of her building. Fortunately, Sandra was much better now, and the only people who knew about her pain-crazed outburst were Val, Malcolm, and Hillary.

In fact, as Val pushed through the door, she saw Sandra sitting at a corner table, her head hidden beneath a voluminous hood, face bent over her sketch pad. Val ordered her customary butterscotch latte and strolled over.

"I'm surprised to see you here."

Sandra started and jerked her head up. Her hood slid back, and she quickly reached to catch it before it fell to her neck. Still, the hood slid far enough for one of her little hair snakes to poke its head out, flickering a pink tongue at Val.

"Oh, Val!" Sandra hastily tucked her hair back in, tugging the hood down over her forehead. Her petrifying eyes were covered by mirrored aviator sunglasses, which reflected Val's own face as Sandra looked up. "You startled me."

"I noticed. I'm surprised to see you here."

"My therapist said I have to forgive myself. Part of that is coming back here like I used to and trying to feel normal again." Sandra dropped her gaze. "Even if I'll never feel normal again."

"You're seeing a therapist? How's that going?"

"It's really good, actually. She's helping me work through what's happened to me. Most of all, she's helping me with the guilt. Accepting that the things that happened to me aren't my fault. That all of this isn't some kind of punishment for my sins or something."

Val's heart clenched. That guilt was a feeling she knew all too well.

"I can give you her address, if you want? I'm sure she could help you too." Sandra's voice was soft and earnest.

Val jerked as if she'd touched a hot stove.

"No thanks. Therapy's not really my thing."

"Have you tried it?"

"Yeah. They made us sit in a circle and talk about our feelings in the loony bin they locked me up in when I was a teenager. I'll pass." Sandra opened her mouth to say more, but Val quickly changed the subject. "Did Hillary talk to you about Malcolm's surprise party?"

Sandra frowned but dropped the subject. She bobbed her head.

"She said you were looking for a venue to host it?"

Val cursed under her breath. "Yeah, though I have no idea why it's my responsibility all of a sudden. Do you have any ideas?"

Sandra shrugged apologetically. "No. This is about the only place I go besides home. Well, this and the library. I'm still getting used to going out in public again. Baby steps."

"The library? Have you still got a crush on the Librarian?"

The gorgon's cheeks flushed scarlet.

"Well… I mean… She's really nice. And she doesn't treat me like a monster…" Sandra stammered.

"I'm just messing with you. If you want to get involved with an ancient godlike being, that's your business. I hope it works out."

*"It certainly seems to have worked out for you, Val,"* Mister E quipped.

"That's debatable," she muttered.

"How is your day going?" Sandra asked.

Val told her about her search for Rosa's nephew, and the shifter girl she'd had to save from a violent mob.

"Pretty much your typical Val Keri day," she concluded. "Full of monsters and mystery."

"Those protests are getting bad," Sandra said. "Mayor Light has really been riling people up. I hear he's giving a speech outside the Mission Shifter Settlement this afternoon."

"Really?" Val blood ran cold. "When?"

"Right now, I think."

Across the shop, the barista called her name. Val was already in motion.

"Thanks, Sandra. It looks like my latte is ready. See you around."

Val took her coffee out into the afternoon drizzle, warm butterscotch coating her tongue as she strode toward the shifter settlement. Unfortunately, she couldn't enjoy the latte. Concern for Alain and the other shifters wiped the taste from her tongue. As she got within a couple of blocks, raised voices echoed off the buildings.

When the settlement finally came into view, she sucked in a breath and swore, "Flying toads."

Before her was a sea of screaming, sign-waving, angry people. The Mission Shifter Settlement was surrounded.

# 10

The chanting sea of protestors outside the settlement made the crowd Val had found attacking the shifter girl in the street look like a friendly potluck. There were hundreds of people jamming the street outside the front gate, holding signs and … cheering? Why were they cheering?

Then she saw the stage that had been erected just outside the gate, and the smiling man stepping up behind the lectern. He had a sharp blue suit, immaculate silver hair, and a million-dollar smile. His blue eyes sparkled like he was sharing an inside joke. A stiff man with a clipboard, a woman in a fur wrap and a pink dress, and a pair of security guards in sharp suits stood behind him.

"Mayor Light," Val breathed.

*"Oh good, the demagogue."* Mister E's tone was full of disgust. *"Just what we need, more fear and hatred."*

Beyond the mayor, the Mission Shifter Settlement looked even more crowded than the last time Val was there. Through the patchwork fence, it resembled a shantytown; tarps and tents and even cardboard-box shelters grew like mushrooms in every nook and cranny. It was a far cry from the cozy little community Val had first visited back when she'd been tracking Ruby's killer.

Dozens of shifters peered out at the protestors through gaps in the fence. They looked thin and malnourished. Their clothing was ragged, hair matted and tangled. They looked like refugees, survivors of some great storm washed up in the Mission. Nothing like the angry mob of well-fed townspeople gathered outside the gate.

"Never underestimate the power of stupid people in large numbers," Val muttered.

She set her jaw in annoyance and started to work her way around the edges of the crowd, hoping she could slip past them and reach the entrance to the settlement. Nobody paid her any attention. They were all focused on Charles Light, their expressions so rapt they might have been hypnotized.

Val did her best to ignore the man's words, but he had a powerful presence. His voice rose and fell as he spoke, the rhythm worming its way into her brain even if the individual words did not. To her surprise, the feeling his speech gave her wasn't one of anger or hatred. Rather, it was one of hope. Light's voice wrapped her in a warm blanket, making her feel safe and protected. There were terrors out there, he seemed to be saying, things too big and scary to handle on your own. But fear not. I will protect you.

"He's good," she admitted. "My brain hates the guy, but my body still responds to him. It doesn't even matter what he's saying. He projects this emotional tide that sweeps you up."

*"I don't think it's the mayor's speech projecting that tide,"* Mister E mused.

"What do you mean?"

*"Look at the crowd. Use my eyes."*

As her vision shifted, Val saw a pale pink force flowing out from the platform, caressing the crowd in gentle waves. Wherever the power touched, people's faces went soft, their eyes shining with adoration.

"He's charming them," Val said. "Is that the power behind the throne?"

*"So it would seem."*

"Let's get a closer look."

Changing course, she pushed her way into the crowd. Despite her applying shoulders and elbows to get by in some places, nobody paid any attention to her passage. The people's enraptured gazes remained fixed on the stage.

The closer she got to the front of the crowd, the harder Val found to tear her eyes away from Charles Light. He deserved her attention. She admired his strong jaw and straight teeth. His melodic baritone voice soothed her like a lullaby. Nothing else mattered.

*"Don't look directly at him. Focus on something else,"* Mister E hissed.

"What?" Val couldn't pull her eyes away from the mayor. The demon-cat's voice sounded very far away.

*"Don't give in to the power. You have to fight it."*

"Fight it?" Val murmured. "Why would I fight?"

Mayor Light was such a handsome man. Tan skin and piercing blue eyes. She could tell he had an athlete's body from the way he filled out that suit. She found herself watching his mouth as he spoke. Imagining the feel of his lips on her skin.

Her temperature started to rise.

Val no longer heard Light's words at all. She just felt his physical presence. The sound of his voice caressed her like rose petals. She didn't understand what all the backlash was about. How could anyone not see? This man was exactly what San Francisco needed. What she needed.

The focus of her entire universe narrowed to Charles Light's face. She basked in his warm presence; he was the sun around which she orbited.

She could no longer hear Mister E at all. She could hear nothing but the voice of Charles Light. Her magical sight flickered on and off, the world alternating between gray reality and cotton candy waves of pink power.

The shifter compound was the problem. She could see that now. The city would be a much better place if it was gone. They would all be happier and safer. They needed to return to a simpler time. A time before monsters stalked the streets.

They needed to tear the settlement down. Wipe it clean and start anew.

As one, the crowd began to move forward.

Hands seized hold of the patchwork fencing surrounding the settlement. Chain link and old boards. Sheets of tin and wavy plastic. They would rip it all down.

Distantly, she noticed the rain was picking up. Rivulets running from her wet hair down over her face.

It didn't matter. Nothing could pull her attention away from Mayor Light.

People were streaming through the gaps in the fence now. Hefting two by fours and baseball bats. Lengths of rebar and rusty pipe. Going in to eradicate the stain on their city. Wipe them all away.

A shifter leapt up onto the platform behind Charles Light, half-transformed, covered in black fur with long canines bared. The shifter launched himself at the mayor, but only got halfway across the platform before he was tackled by a policeman wearing black body armor.

Light's voice faltered as his security detail hustled him away from the podium. The warmth caressing the crowd flickered and died. The sun went out.

Val shivered as she became aware of the cold rain running down the back of her neck.

Then she noticed the screaming.

Armed protestors flooded into the shifter settlement through the destroyed fence. Desperate shifters were fighting back. The air was sharp with the scent of blood.

# 11

Val waded into chaos. Protestors with pipes and baseball bats tore through the settlement. They were ripping down the shifters' makeshift walls and roofs, baring their tattered blankets and meager possessions to the rain. Some of the shifters ran. Others tried to stop the mob and were swept aside. A few fought back.

The most desperate shifted.

Val saw a young mother cornered, tears running down her face as she tried to protect a small boy with her body. A well-dressed man grabbed her by the hair and yanked her away from the child. The mother went berserk, shifting in the space of an indrawn breath, becoming all claws and fur and teeth. The man's blood splattered in hot ribbons, painting the shantytown's walls. The young mother turned and snarled at the crowd, an enormous badger now, her teeth long and sharp and dipped in red. For a moment, the crowd drew back.

Then they let out a cry of rage and descended on her in a tide of fists and boots and bats.

Val didn't know what to do. Everywhere she turned, she was surrounded by violence. Protestors beating shifters. Shifters lashing out at protestors. All of them caught up in a red haze of fear and rage, snarling and screaming, contorted so badly none of them looked human anymore.

Her own anger and frustration rose to meet them.

It was spinning out of control, and she didn't know how to stop it. Sure, she could fight. She was good at that. But that was what everyone else was doing. What they needed was less fighting, not more.

But she didn't know what else to do. And she had to try.

Her fingers curled into fists.

"Baby steps," she growled. "One atrocity at a time."

Turning to the crowd attacking the young mother, Val summoned a tight little whirlwind. It sucked up dust and small pebbles and puddles as it spun, quickly becoming a weird combination of dust devil and waterspout. She turned it on the people attacking the badger-woman and they fell away, spitting out water as they shielded their eyes and faces. It was surprisingly effective.

*"Now I see why they turn fire hoses on riots."* Mister E smiled his crescent moon smile.

Val knelt beside the young mother. She had reverted to her human form and lay on the ground, badly beaten. Unconscious but alive.

She gently pulled the woman back beneath the corner of a wavy tin roof, where she would be out of the way and somewhat protected from the elements. She looked up to find the little boy staring at her with wide eyes.

"She's going to be OK." Val hoped she wasn't lying. "Can you stay here and watch over her while she's sleeping?"

The boy nodded solemnly and sat beside his mother, cradling her bloody head in his hands. Val wished she could do more for the woman, but she wasn't a healer. The shifter was bruised and bleeding from dozens of shallow wounds, but none appeared life threatening. At least the woman wasn't lying in a puddle of blood and didn't appear to be dying at that moment, which was the limit of Val's medical diagnosis abilities. Shifters tended to heal pretty quickly. She had to trust that would be enough.

She gave the boy a tight smile and turned back to the chaos. The rain was coming down hard now, so thick she had to squint to see through it. Her mouth dropped open in dismay. Where to even begin? The settlement was in shambles. Everywhere she looked, people were tearing down shelters. Shifters fought and bled.

To her right she saw a familiar black dog holding off a group of three men. Alain! The dog shifter was the leader of the settlement, and a good friend. She took a step toward him, but the crowd surged between them, cutting her off.

Frustration constricted her throat, making it hard to breathe. It was too much. If she continued breaking up fights one at a time, there would be nothing left of the settlement. But how could she blow down the entire mob without also blowing down the settlement?

She tried her whirlwind-waterspout trick on a knot of people cornering a small woman wrapped in a ragged blanket — but felt the futility of her actions even as the tactic once again succeeded. It was too slow. If she continued to break up the fights one by one, the settlement would be flattened before she stopped even half the mob.

The rain intensified again, becoming a physical presence, the weight of it pressing down like the hand of a giant, so thick that the world became a blur. The shapes of the people around her softened into watercolor smears. Several of them fell to their knees, even as she stubbornly braced herself against the downpour, refusing to go down.

*"This isn't a natural rain,"* Mister E hissed. *"Someone is doing this."*

"You think?" Val grunted, teeth grinding together as she braced her weight against her knees. It felt like an 18-wheeler was parked on her back. Like she was standing under Niagara Falls. "Tell me something I don't know."

The rain turned to sleet, little balls of ice hammering down. She raised her arms, trying to protect her head with her leather jacket. In doing so, she lost her bracing, and the weight of the water became too great. She fell heavily onto her hip and shoulder. Drawing her knees to her chest, Val curled into a protective ball.

The hailstones were getting larger. They hurt.

"I feel like a steak getting tenderized," Val groaned.

She made a little shield of air over her body, deflecting the balls of ice away. Just in time too, as a ball of ice the size of a walnut bounced off the ground right in front of her face. All around her, people were screaming and diving for shelter. She saw a young woman take a hail-stone to the temple and crumple, a marionette with cut strings. Others were on the ground all around, too injured to get to shelter.

Val's eyes widened as she saw Alain. He was half shifted, a naked man covered in thick black fur, lying face down in the mud.

She crawled in his direction, extending her air shield over his prone form, hoping she wasn't too late. Icy fingers of dread encircled her throat as she reached his body. He was so still. She pressed shaking fingers to his skin.

Warm relief rushed through her. Alain had a pulse.

She sensed someone behind her and turned.

"You. I should have known," she snarled.

The shadowy presence from the mob scene that morning stood there. The man in the rain. The one who'd drowned all those people. The one who'd tried to drown her.

Val pushed herself to her feet and stepped toward him. She still couldn't see him clearly. His features were obscured by a shimmering curtain of water.

"Who are you?" she asked.

He regarded her silently for so long that she wondered if he even had a voice.

Then he spoke.

"I am the Rain King."

# 12

V al stared hard at the Rain King, trying to see the man behind the veil of water. He seemed to be wearing a long black trench coat and hat of some kind. Possibly a fedora. His features were invisible beneath the brim, and everything about him was dark and blurred, like a charcoal sketch gone soft at the edges. The hail had turned back to rain, and he smelled strongly of it, along with something else.

It took Val a minute to figure out what she was inhaling wasn't a scent at all, but an emotion. Sadness. It came off him in a wave so thick it almost choked her.

"That's the second time today you've tried to kill me," Val snarled. "You killed a bunch of those protestors earlier. Tell me why I shouldn't kick your ass right now."

The man cocked his head at her as if she were speaking a foreign language.

"The city must have peace," he said.

"Peace? How does murdering a bunch of people bring peace?"

*"You of all people should know the answer to that one,"* Mister E said.

Val ignored him, but even as the words left her lips, she already knew the answer. Moments ago, the settlement had been engulfed in a bloody riot. Now it was silent and still; the only sounds left were the patter of the rain and the cries of the wounded.

"Answer me!" she barked.

The Rain King indicated Alain, lying motionless at her feet. "Would you prefer I let them kill each other? Would that be better?"

"I would prefer it if no one killed anyone."

The Rain King shrugged.

"That is not an option."

"I had it under control. I was going to stop them."

"No. You weren't."

Val stepped forward, fists clenched, shaking with rage.

"This is my city. I won't let you go around killing people."

"Do you think you can stop me?" The Rain King sounded amused.

In response, Val summoned another whirlwind. She made it big this time, a full ten feet across. It circled around the Rain King, penning him inside its swirling walls.

He made no response at first. He simply stood there, an indistinct figure behind the swirling wind.

Then the heavens opened up.

The rain hit Val so hard it felt like someone had opened a gigantic tap in the sky. Like the entire bay was coming down on her head all at once. She staggered beneath the falling water and was slammed to the ground. Her whirlwind disappeared, but Val didn't even notice. She was too busy trying not to drown.

She turned her face away from the deluge, but the water clung to her skin, defying gravity as it wrapped itself over her nose and mouth. She tried to wipe it away, but it flowed around her fingers. Her lungs burned with the need for oxygen.

In desperation, Val lashed out at the Rain King. She couldn't see more than vague shadows and light through the water, but she thought she could tell where the figure stood. She sent fists of wind in that direction, probing blindly, praying she might distract him.

Her first punch missed. Her second did as well.

Her lungs spasmed, nearly forcing her to suck in water. She had only seconds left.

She threw out dozens of windy fists, spraying them out in a

desperate arc, a heavyweight champion barrage of blows, one after another, a machine gun spray-and-pray.

Finally, something must have connected because the water dropped away from her face. Val sucked in ragged gulps of air as the rain slackened, until it was simply a normal mist falling once more.

When she looked up, the Rain King was gone.

"That's right. You'd better run," she croaked, dragging herself to her feet, teeth bared in a grim smile.

Twenty minutes later, she wasn't smiling anymore.

Alain turned out to be mostly fine. He was thoroughly battered and bruised, but his shifter healing powers would take care of those quickly enough.

The good news ended there.

The carnage in the shifter settlement was worse than she'd feared. Nearly half of the ramshackle shelters had been torn down, and over a dozen shifters had been beaten to death by Mayor Light's crazed followers. An equal number of protestors had been wounded or killed.

And that was only the beginning of the body count. Nearly twice as many people had been killed by the Rain King. Bludgeoned by hailstones or drowned.

Val worked somberly next to Alain, pulling bodies from collapsed shelters. Laying them in neat rows on the muddy ground.

"These people came here for protection." Tears ran down Alan's face as he gently closed the eyes of a lifeless young woman. Her drowned face was pale and bloated. "All they wanted was a safe place to live in peace."

"I think that's all any of us want, really," Val said.

"That's bullshit, Val. If all we wanted was peace, we would have peace. These people"—he gestured to the remnants of Mayor Light's mob—"didn't want peace. They hated and feared us because we were different. They wanted to destroy us."

"It looks like they got a little more destruction than they bargained for."

"Why?" Alain turned to her, his eyes brimming with tears. "Why do they hate us? We don't hurt them. Why can't they just leave us alone?" The shifter leader looked terrified and exhausted. On the verge of despair. Val had never seen him so low.

Alain's words tugged at her heart. She wished she had an answer that made sense, but all she could do was raise her hands in a helpless shrug.

"I don't know. People fear the things they don't understand. Maybe it's some kind of primitive survival instinct we haven't evolved past. What I do know is that these people's fear wouldn't have turned into violence if it wasn't for Mayor Light. He transformed that fear into hatred, and directed that hatred towards your settlement. He's got some kind of power that hypnotizes people. I felt it myself. That man is extremely dangerous."

"Can you stop him?"

"I don't know. He's the mayor. I'm not sure what I can do against someone that powerful. That's above my pay grade."

"What about the other one? The Rain King. He murdered my people as well."

Val grimaced.

"I don't know about him yet. This was the second time today I've seen him drown one of Mayor Light's demonstrations that turned violent. He clearly doesn't like Light's people any more than we do."

"But he killed my people too!"

"Yeah, I know. I can't figure out what his angle is. He said something about the city needing peace. His motives seem complicated." Val sighed and set her jaw. "I guess the bottom line is: He's a killer. I'll track him down and stop him if I can."

# 13

Val returned to the Imaginarium with a heavy heart. As she navigated the labyrinthine halls, she kept seeing dead and wounded shifters in her mind. People who had been transformed by a magic they had neither asked for nor understood. Who had been persecuted by their friends and family, forced to flee from their homes and take refuge in the Mission Shifter Settlement. People who had already lost the safety they'd once enjoyed. Now they'd not only lost the dubious protection of the settlement, but many had lost their lives as well.

She sat on a stump in a corner of Feather's garden beside a spreading fern, watching the students file in for the music class. Most didn't even notice her sitting there. They talked excitedly amongst themselves. Smiling. Absorbed in their own worlds. Unaware that just blocks away people's homes and lives had been destroyed.

Feather flitted around the garden, bright and lively as she checked in with each of her students. Val noticed that she was a toucher — often laying a hand on a student's arm or shoulder when addressing them.

Val shuddered. As someone who didn't like to be touched, Feather was pretty much her worst nightmare.

Finally, the students all settled into the music circle and class began. Feather's teaching method wasn't what Val had envisioned in a music class at all. In her mind, music was a solitary pursuit that involved long hours of sitting and practicing alone. Feather's class was more focused on playing music together, and with enthusiasm. Even when her students flubbed their part, Feather was always supportive and encouraging. The little woman's smile never left her face.

"See, teachers don't have to be so grumpy," Val muttered under her breath.

Mister E snorted.

*"Are you listening to this so-called music? A band of deaf leopards could play better. If you want your magic to work as poorly as this music does, then I can blow glitter and rainbows up your ass all you want."*

He did have a point. While the students were clearly enjoying themselves, the result was ... not great.

When the class finally ended, Feather drifted over to Val's stump.

"Did you enjoy the music?" she asked, reaching out to take Val's hand.

Val jerked the hand away, hiding it inside the pocket of her leather jacket.

"The music was ... interesting." She was proud of her diplomacy.

Feather beamed.

"It's not about the result, you know. Life is a journey, and we're all at different places in our process. I believe it's counterproductive to get down on yourself for not being perfect. We can't all be Mozart or Leonard Cohen. I tell my students to appreciate the music, wherever they are on their musical journey. Even if the only thing you can do is strum a single chord, or bang a drum, or hum the melody, you are still making music, and you should celebrate and enjoy that. Maybe next year you'll be a virtuoso playing beautiful complicated solos. Maybe not. Either way, the important thing is to enjoy where you are today, and not worry so much about where you might be tomorrow."

Despite Val's skepticism, Feather's words made sense. She knew from her own martial and magical training that, no matter how much she improved, there were always higher levels of mastery to strive for. She was never as good as she wanted to be. This made her feel perpetually restless and unfulfilled. Maybe she needed to learn to relax and accept where she was on her journey?

*"Learn to accept being bad at something,"* Mister E scoffed. *"That sounds like a recipe for never becoming a master to me."*

"She's not saying to accept being bad at something," Val muttered. "She's saying to not beat yourself up about not being as good as you want to be yet."

*"And while you're learning, you're OK with being bad. Sounds like a lazy rationalization for never practicing."*

"You can practice six hours a day and still not be good at something. Learning takes time."

*"So you enjoy being mediocre. I understand perfectly."*

Val made a strangled sound in her throat.

Feather blinked at her uncertainly.

"Are you all right?"

"Fine." Val forced a tight smile. "Just arguing with myself. It's not important."

The little woman returned the smile brightly.

"Oh, yes. I do that all the time. The best part about arguing with yourself is that you always win."

"If only that were true." Val sighed as she felt Mister E grin.

"So, how can I help you?" Feather asked.

"You said you were going to introduce me to some of Jorge's classmates."

"Yes, of course!"

Val followed the teacher to a small group of students who stood chatting.

"Students, this is Val Keri. She has some questions for you." The little woman excused herself with a smile. "I'll leave you to it."

Val surveyed the group. There were two men and three women, ranging in age from about twenty to sixty. Other than their enthusiasm for music, they didn't appear to have much in common. The men were middle-aged, one a working-class guy in a flannel shirt, the other a sharply dressed gay man with an expensive haircut. Two of the women were yoga-pants types wearing spotless sneakers.

The final woman was the youngest, a girl with black-coffee skin who seemed to be in her early twenties. She had dyed blue hair that cascaded off one side of her head in a wave. Her clothes were ragged and full of holes, but not in a way that suggested poverty; it was more as if she just didn't pay any attention to her clothing. Her nails were bitten to the quick and she had nervous fingers that toyed with the ragged fringe on her oversized sweater. But she stood with her feet planted solidly, and her dark eyes met Val's with a challenge.

Val decided to be direct.

"As you may have heard, Jorge is missing. His family has asked me to find him. I'm hoping you can help. Can you tell me when you last saw him?"

The men and yoga-pants women exchanged glances, their eyes drifting toward the younger woman. The blue-haired girl looked away, becoming more invested in unravelling her sweater.

When the silence had stretched to an uncomfortable length, the gay man cleared his throat.

"It's been a couple of weeks since Jorge came to class."

"There's a bar we all go to after class sometimes," one of the yoga pants chimed in. She had dark eyes and the kind of curly hair it would take a steamroller to flatten. "The Green Garden. I think we all went there the last time he came to class."

"That's right, we did," the other yoga pants agreed. "I think it was maybe three weeks ago?"

"That sounds right," expensive haircut said.

Their eyes all drifted to the younger woman again, as if waiting for her to speak. She didn't, nor did she look up from her sweater.

"Did you notice anything unusual about him that day?" Val asked. "Was he acting differently in any way?"

"Well … hmmm." Flannel shirt grimaced.

"Not that I noticed," the curly-haired woman said, her eyes darting to the younger woman like a fish jumping upstream. She was a terrible liar.

Val decided to stop beating around the bush.

"Is there anything you'd like to add?" she asked the blue-haired woman directly.

She flinched as if Val had slapped her. The girl bit her lip, her eyes welling up. A single tear rolled down her cheek.

"We broke up that day," she said.

# 14

"*Oh, now it's getting juicy,*" Mister E crowed. *"Love stories always make the best tragic tales."*

Val was glad no one else could hear the insensitive cat.

"Can you tell me your name?" she asked the girl.

"Miranda."

"Miranda, can you tell me about the last time you saw Jorge?"

Miranda nodded without looking up, her fingers still shredding the end of her sleeve. She looked miserable and unhealthy, like she hadn't slept or eaten properly in weeks.

"We went to the Green Garden after class," she began. "All of us did. Jorge was quiet that night. He'd been dealing with some family stuff for a few weeks and he was angry and depressed. I tried to get him to talk to me about it, but he wouldn't. He just became more withdrawn."

Miranda stopped talking and fixated on her sweater sleeve again.

"Do you know what kind of family stuff?" Val prompted.

Miranda sighed as if she really didn't want to talk about it. But after a beat, she reluctantly continued, "It had to do with his sister. Something about her husband? Or maybe her landlord? I'm really not sure. Like I said, he didn't want to talk about it."

Another tear ran down the girl's cheek. She didn't seem to notice.

"Anyway, that night he was upset. Something had made him really pissed off. I tried to get him to tell me what was wrong, to talk to me, but he just snapped. He screamed at me. Said this wasn't working out and he didn't have time to waste on 'us.' That he had more important things to do." Miranda's voice had thickened, her body vibrating with barely suppressed anger. The curly-haired woman stepped up and put her arms around the girl, but Miranda shrugged her off.

Val stood there awkwardly, unsure what to do. Comforting people was not her strong suit. And the girl's classmates seemed to have the comforting part covered anyway. She exchanged helpless looks with the two men, who looked just as awkward and uncomfortable as she did.

Thankfully, Miranda recovered quickly. She angrily swiped the sleeve of her sweater across her eyes and shrugged away from the curly-haired woman.

"I'm sorry," she said.

"No, that's completely understandable," Val said. "So what happened after that?"

Miranda looked down at her sweater. "He left."

"That's it? Did you see him again after that?"

"No. That was the last time I saw him. He hasn't been back to class since. I stopped by his apartment one day to see if he was OK, but he didn't answer."

"Is there anything else you can tell me? Did Jorge have any enemies? Anyone who might want to hurt him?"

"Not that I know of." The girl folded her arms across her chest and met Val's gaze defiantly. She was clearly done talking.

Any of you? Any ideas where he might have gone?" Val's eyes met each of theirs in turn. They all shook their heads.

"OK, well here's my card." Val handed out the cards Malcolm had designed and printed for her. She felt like an imposter as she scanned the flowing silver ink: *Valora Keri, Private Investigator - Strange Activities Specialist*. The cards had been Malcolm's idea, as had the title.

Really, now that she thought about it, the entire thing was Malcolm's fault.

"Except for the sticking-your-nose-into-trouble part," she muttered to herself. "You do that just fine on your own."

To the others, she said, "Thank you for your help. If any of you think of anything else that might help me find Jorge, please let me know." Her eyes lingered on Miranda, but the girl only gave her a flat stare in return.

As she headed out into the rain, Mister E immediately said, *"She's lying."*

"Yeah, I thought so too. She got cagey there at the end, when she said she hadn't seen him again after that night."

*"Maybe she killed him. Hell hath no fury like a woman scorned."*

"I don't know that angry ex-lover necessarily equals murder, but I suppose it's possible. But you are right about one thing: There's definitely something she isn't telling us."

Val's turned Miranda's words over in her head. *"He'd been dealing with some family stuff ... It had to do with his sister ... her husband ... Or maybe her landlord?"*

She needed to dig deeper, and it seemed the mystery was circling back to the place where it began: Jorge's family. After all, they were the ones who had put her on this case to begin with. Specifically, his aunt, who was apparently having prophetic dreams.

It was time to go talk to Rosa.

# 15

Val found Rosa in her usual place, working behind the counter in the little market on the corner. Val stood outside under the green awning, pretending to peruse the fruit in the wooden crates as she watched Rosa through the open door. Her friend was wrapped in a turquoise hoodie, dealing with a small line of people grabbing groceries or fresh tamales for their dinner. She chatted with her customers as she worked, smiling and friendly. In her element.

But Val saw the dark half-moons beneath her eyes that she'd tried to conceal with makeup. The way her smile cracked at the corners. Rosa's happy shopkeeper facade was a thin veneer, held together with scotch tape and caffeine. It was obvious she wasn't sleeping well.

Val waited until the last customers had walked off clutching their purchases and Rosa had flipped the OPEN sign to SHUT. Then, when she thought nobody was watching, Rosa dropped the facade and sagged against the counter. She was exhausted, sustained solely by the stubborn will to keep going.

She leaned against the counter for a long moment, head down, taking deep breaths. Then she gathered herself and stepped outside to bring in the produce crates for the evening.

Rosa jumped and gave a little squeak when she saw Val standing there.

"Val Keri, you nearly gave me a heart attack."

"I bet you say that to all the girls."

Rosa grimaced and picked up a crate of apples. Val grabbed a crate of bananas and followed her inside.

"I don't have time to say anything to any girls these days. Besides, girls get freaked out when you wake up screaming in the middle of the night."

"You're still having bad dreams?"

"Every night. Sometimes more than one. I can't remember the last time I got a full night's sleep."

"Do you want to tell me about them?"

Rosa sighed and rubbed her bloodshot eyes. "They're all different, but certain things come up over and over. The one I see most often is rain."

Val glanced at the glistening street. "Rain isn't exactly a rare occurrence these days. It seems pretty natural you'd dream about it."

"Yeah, but this rain is different."

"Different how?"

"Well, first of all, it's usually made of blood."

Val raised an eyebrow. "That's certainly different. Anything else?"

"I see my nephew sometimes. And Mayor Light."

"Mayor Light?" Val's head jerked up. "That asshole is definitely creating blood rain. I've had two confrontations with his supporters in the last twenty-four hours. He had a rally outside the Mission Shifter Settlement this afternoon that turned into a riot. His followers stormed the settlement and started beating shifters to death. I tried to stop them, but there were too many. Then this Rain King guy showed up and told everyone to chill out with hailstones."

"Rain King?"

Val waved the name away. "Some psycho who thinks that large scale slaughter is the secret to crowd control."

Rosa nodded, digesting this before asking, "Have you found Jorge yet?"

"No, but I think I'm making progress. That's what I stopped by to talk to you about." Val filled Rosa in on what Miranda had told her about Jorge's sister and her landlord. "Do you know anything about that?"

Rosa shook her head. "No, that's the first I've heard about it."

"Can you put me in touch with his sister?"

"I can give you her address. She lives out by the old zoo."

Val grimaced at that. Things in that part of the city were ... interesting. The Sunset neighborhoods west of Twin Peaks had become harder to access thanks to roads collapsing and crevices opening up. The old zoo area in particular had been heavily damaged in the big quake and fallen into anarchy. From what Val had heard, it was pretty dangerous, with gangs and cultists running wild.

She put on a brave smile.

"I guess I'll just have to be careful. Tell me where I need to go. Then you go home and get some rest. You look like you were tied to a bumper and dragged for three miles."

"Awww, you're so sweet." Rosa stepped forward and gave her a quick hug that made Val stiffen, and not just because she didn't enjoy being touched. Rosa had lost a lot of weight. Val could feel her friend's bones pressing against her skin. "You don't look so fresh yourself. You can't find Jorge if you're so tired you step out in front of a truck. Get some rest yourself, Val. The world will still be here tomorrow."

Val huffed a laugh.

"That's exactly what I'm afraid of."

# 16

Val rolled out of bed and followed her nose to the kitchen, where coffee was already brewing. Malcolm stood at the stove wearing a yellow apron with a picture of a surly goose on it that read, 'Bitch, I'm cooking.' She poured herself a cup of the good stuff, added a liberal dose of butterscotch creamer, and slumped into a chair at the table.

"Good morning, sunshine," Malcolm said. "Chocolate pancakes will be ready in a few minutes."

"Why?" Val asked.

"Why what? Why will they be ready in a few minutes? Or why am I cooking?"

"Cooking." Val took a big slurp of her coffee. She couldn't manage more than one word at a time until the caffeine hit her system.

"I'm cooking because I love to cook. You know that."

"You eat?" Two words. Things were looking up.

"I don't need to eat anymore, no. But I do like to eat. Being undead isn't all dusty coffins and pasty skin, you know. A girl's got to live a little. Pancakes are one of the things that make life worth living."

"Mmmm."

Malcolm took Val's lack of verbosity in stride. He knew the way she was in the morning.

"Have you seen the living room? We've got the walls all torn out. Everything is down to the studs."

"I saw. Well done." Four words now. The coffee was definitely starting to nudge things along.

"We're going to get all the debris cleared out and start putting up the new walls today."

Val raised an eyebrow. "You can put up walls?"

"Well, I never have before, but I'm plenty strong now. I just need some direction." He struck a pose and flexed biceps that looked no more impressive than they ever had, which was to say not very impressive at all, before slapping a plate down in front of her. "Here. Have some pancakes."

"Thank you." Val busied herself with the butter and syrup. "Who is doing the directing?"

"That would be me." Gunter Gristle ducked his shaggy head in through the doorway. The troll's bulky form filled it completely. He held out an empty mug. "Got any more coffee?"

"Gunter? What are you doing here?" Val asked.

"Directing," Malcolm said as he refilled Gunter's mug. "We already covered that. Try to keep up, Val."

Val side-eyed the big troll as he retreated to the living room.

"I didn't realize you knew Gunter."

"Girl, please. I know everyone."

Val couldn't argue with that. He certainly knew a lot more people than she did.

"Good morning." Sandra slipped into the kitchen and made a beeline for the coffee pot. Her snake-hair was concealed beneath the oversized hood of her fox onesie, her deadly eyes hidden behind the ever-present mirrored aviator sunglasses.

Val stared. "Does everyone live here now?"

"Cool your jets. I invited her up for chocolate pancakes," Malcolm said. He heaped another plate and handed it to Sandra, who meekly took the seat across from Val at the table.

Val wanted to glare at Malcolm, but it was hard to stay mad at him with a mouth full of pancakes. So she glared at Sandra instead. Unfortunately, thanks to Sandra's mirrored glasses, that meant her own reflection glared right back at her, which made her feel silly. She shifted her gaze to her coffee mug instead.

"The only one missing is Hillary," she grumbled.

"You're welcome to go wake her up if you like," Malcolm said. "I wouldn't recommend it, though. She sleeps like the dead."

"No thank you. I'd rather keep all my limbs attached."

"Smart girl. How's the search for Rosa's nephew going?"

"Not great."

"Do tell."

So she did, filling him in on the events of the previous day. When she'd finished, Malcolm tapped a manicured fingernail against his lips.

"It sounds like you're making reasonable progress on finding Jorge. You've got a good lead, anyway."

"It's a lead. I don't know if I'd call it good."

"What I want to know is: Who is this Rain King character? He sounds dangerous and mysterious. Just my type, really. Is he cute?"

"I couldn't see his face through all the rain," Val said dryly. "And did you miss the part where he's a psychotic mass murderer? I don't see anything cute about that."

"Sure, but he was murdering Mayor Light's minions, which is justifiable homicide in my book."

"A bunch of shifters died too."

"Problematic," he acknowledged. "But not necessarily a deal breaker."

"You're impossible."

"No, I'm easy," he corrected with a smirk. "But in all seriousness, I feel like there's a connection here. You should look into this Rain King guy more."

"I'm a little busy trying to find Jorge. But if you want to take that on, be my guest. Maybe you could take a trip to the Library and see what comes up. Look under 'R' for Rain."

"Stick to your day job, Val. Leave the jokes to the professionals." Malcolm scooped the last of the chocolate pancakes onto a plate and joined them at the table, using the low kitchen stool for a seat. "I'd be happy to go to the Library, but in case you've forgotten, I'm a little busy reconstructing the living room. Also, it's daytime, and while I'm not one of those vampires who likes to sleep all day, I also prefer not to go outside if I can help it. It's bad for my skin."

"Convenient."

Malcolm smiled brightly. "Isn't it, though? But Sandra could go to the Library for you."

Sandra choked on her pancakes.

"Me?" she squeaked, once she'd finished coughing. "I don't think I'm very good at research."

"You don't have to be," Malcolm insisted. "You just need to ask the Librarian for assistance."

Sandra's cheeks turned cherry red.

"You know you want to," he continued without mercy.

"I… uh… Can't you come with me?"

"Can and should are too different things. I could come with you, but should I? I've got other things to do." He winked. "And I wouldn't want to mess with your mojo."

"Please? We can stop at Brownie's Bakery on the way. I'll buy you a chocolate croissant."

Malcolm sighed dramatically.

"Fine. I suppose I can get out my day gear and Gunter can put up walls by himself for a while. But only because you bribed me so nicely. You know I can't resist Brownie's."

"Thank you." The relief in Sandra's voice was palpable.

"It's settled then. Sandra and I will go ask the Librarian about the Rain King. Val will talk to Jorge's sister. And Gunter will stay here and put up new walls in the living room." Malcolm beamed. "I love it when a plan comes together."

Val rolled her eyes and poured herself another cup of coffee.

# 17

W hen the big quake hit San Francisco, the area south of Twin Peaks descended into something straight out of a nightmare. Several hillsides collapsed, burying Portola Drive in jagged debris and making it impossible to get out to the Sunset through the canyon. The area between Glen Canyon and John McLaren Park was flattened, and traffic on the 280 Freeway fell off dramatically. Multiple lanes of asphalt became overkill, to say the least. People whose houses had been destroyed started reclaiming the empty acreage in the unused freeway lanes, at first slapping up hasty shelters along the guardrails, then later expanding them into more elaborate permanent structures.

Since the freeway was separated, the logical way to do this would have been to convert half of the freeway entirely to residential use, and to keep either the northbound or southbound lanes free for car and cart traffic.

*"Of course that's not what people did,"* Mister E said.

"No one ever accused people of being logical," Val agreed.

They were trudging along the northbound lanes, which had become crowded with houses and shops two lanes deep. Well, Val was trudging. Mister E floated along on his back, invisible to everyone but Val, striped tail curling and flicking.

The center lane of the freeway was still open for cart and vehicle traffic, though instead of flowing in an orderly one-way manner as traffic had before the Collapse, vehicles now moved in both directions. The hodge-podge construction had crowded the open lane so closely that whenever two carts met traveling in opposite directions, one had to pull to the side to let the other pass in an awkward dance. This sometimes led to memorable shouting matches.

"My feet hurt. I really miss the Ural," Val mourned.

*"Walking is good for you. It builds character."*

"Says the cat who floats everywhere."

Mister E smirked and blew another smoke ring.

The Ural, Val's sturdy old tank of a motorcycle, had been run off the Van Ness bridge by vampires and fallen to an ignominious end in the depths of the Mission Street chasm. Val had considered hauling the old bike out and trying to get it fixed, but she'd given up on that idea after a hike down to visit the wreckage. The Ural had hit the wall of the chasm and tumbled, scattering parts as it went, before the remains of the chassis crumpled against the bottom like an old aluminum can. Melting it down and reforging it would be easier than attempting to repair it at this point.

It was the end of an era. They'd been through a lot together, and Val felt the loss of the old motorcycle deeply. Though, at the moment, she mostly felt her aching feet.

*"You could always fly,"* Mister E suggested.

"I don't think flaunting the fact that I'm a witch in broad daylight is the smartest thing to do. Especially considering the way public sentiment has been moving against all things supernatural."

*"Coward."*

Val turned her collar up against the chill ocean breeze and frowned as she approached a line of carts ahead of them. She walked to the last of the cart drivers sitting hunched under the misty, blustery drizzle.

"What's the holdup?" she called up to a gaunt man wearing a floppy hat.

"Toll booth," he answered in a bored tone.

"Toll booth?" Val repeated under her breath as she strode forward, passing the carts on the right. "Who charges a toll? Nobody owns the freeway, do they?"

As she approached the front of the line, the answer became clear. Someone had rigged a barrier across the road — it looked like a fallen telephone pole mounted on a pivot so it could be raised and lowered. Burly guards stood around the barrier, armed with clubs and knives. They wore blue sashes tied around their arms in what seemed like an attempt at a uniform. One of them even held a nasty-looking assault rifle.

Carts were lined up on both sides of the barrier. On Val's side, the toll collector was arguing with the woman driving the cart at the front of the line. Her cart was fashioned from the bed of a rusty old pickup truck, though the cab and engine had been replaced by a simple wooden bench attached to a pair of mules. A grubby-faced child, maybe three years old, gender indeterminate, sat on the bench beside the woman. The woman was pretty but rail thin, her blond hair wispy, torso wrapped in layers of tattered sweaters. She was pleading with the toll collector, though the stone-faced man appeared unmoved.

Val wondered if she should help the woman but quickly discarded the idea. This wasn't her turf, and she didn't know these people. This sort of discussion probably happened every day. Better to let things take their natural course.

She shook her head as she started to circle around the barrier. Society had collapsed and, instead of banding together, people had just found new ways to take advantage of each other.

"Maybe we're all doomed," she muttered.

One of the guards stepped into her path.

"Where do you think you're going?" he asked.

"The zoo," Val answered. "Though I don't know why it matters to you."

"Back of the line." He pointed a thick finger.

"I'm not driving a cart. I'm walking."

"Back of the line. Everyone has to pay the toll."

Val peered at the unmoving line, which had now grown by three more carts.

"I'm walking," she tried to keep her tone level and reasonable. "Isn't there a pedestrian gate?"

"Nope. Back of the line."

Val ground her teeth and did her best to remain calm.

"How much is the toll?"

"Five chips."

"Chips? What are chips?"

The guard looked at her like she was an idiot.

"Local currency."

"I don't live in this area."

"The money changer is over there." He pointed to a small wooden stall. Val was unsurprised to see the same blue-sashed guards standing guard outside it.

"Reasonable exchange rates, I'm sure," she growled.

"This freeway's the only open road out to the south Sunset. If you want to get to the zoo, you've got to pay. If you don't want to pay, SF is back that way." The guard sneered at her.

"This is bullshit."

"If you don't have the chips, we can arrange alternate payment." The guard leered, running his eyes up and down her body.

"You're disgusting."

"That's the way it works. She's arranging payment right now." He shrugged and gestured to the blonde woman, who had pulled her cart to the side and was now reluctantly following a guard to a shack beside the toll booth. Her face was pale, her eyes blinking back tears.

Val's blood boiled.

"Oh no, you don't," she whispered.

The ocean breeze abruptly strengthened into a proper wind, howling across the surface of the road, pushing the rain sideways. A particularly strong gust hit the guard leading the woman toward the shack, knocking him off his feet and rolling him across the wet pavement.

Val's eyes shone as she gathered the power of the storm. Her skin tingled and her hair rose from her scalp.

The world turned white as lighting struck the barrier in a blinding flash. The telephone pole exploded with a roar, sending wood chips flying and the closest guards sprawling. The stubby remnant of the barrier was engulfed in flames.

Val strode forward and grabbed the blonde woman by the arm.

"Get on your cart," she said. "Go."

The woman looked dazed, her gaze turning from Val to the destroyed barrier and back again.

Val shook her.

"There's no time. Go before the guards get their shit together."

The woman's eyes hardened, lips pressing into a thin line. She nodded and ran to her cart.

"Move out!" Val shouted to the line of carts, before turning and running past the shattered and burning remnant herself.

Curiously, even though the air continued to howl along the edges of the road, pummeling the guards and keeping them pinned down, the breeze was barely a whisper in the traffic lane. Val spat in the direction of the nearest guard lying on the ground as she led the cart drivers right through the destroyed barrier.

# 18

"Hop on!" the blonde woman driving the cart called out. Val didn't need to be told twice. She reached and swung herself up onto the wooden bench seat, settling down on the other side of the child.

"Thank you." She nodded to the woman. "My feet are killing me."

"It's faster than walking." The woman extended a hand. "I'm Helen."

"Val."

"And this is Summer." The woman ruffled the child's hair. The little girl paid no mind, her gaze focused on a small wooden dog in her hands.

Val stared at the girl for a long moment, something catching in her gut as memory flooded her. Summer reminded her of Maddy, her friend Ruby's daughter. The little girl who had been made into an orphan when Ruby was murdered.

Ruby had been a dancer at the Alley Cat, and secretly a shifter, a fact Val hadn't discovered until she was investigating Ruby's murder. Ruby and Maddy had lived in a little cottage in the Mission Shifter Settlement, back when the settlement was still a cute community, and not the overcrowded shantytown it had become now.

Her mind flashed to Mayor Light's mob attacking the shifter settlement, angry humans beating shifters with bats and lengths of pipe.
The Rain King pummeling people with hailstones. All the dead and
injured lying on the ground afterward.

She swallowed past the guilt burning a hole in her gut. She hadn't
thought to check on Maddy afterwards. She hoped the girl was all
right.

Helen said something that Val didn't catch. She yanked her attention back to the present.

"I'm sorry, what was that?"

"I said it's a long walk to the Sunset." Helen repeated. "Where are
you headed?"

"Near the old zoo."

"We're heading past there. I can drop you off at Lake Merced."

"Perfect."

They road in silence for a few minutes. Val could feel Helen
studying her out of the corner of her eye.

Finally, the woman cleared her throat. "That was some scene back
there. I can't believe lightning struck that barrier."

"Yeah," Val agreed. "That was really something."

She could feel Helen weighing her response. Val kept her eyes
forward, playing dumb. She didn't know this woman. Most people
didn't react favorably to witches, so she'd tried to be discreet with her
magic when she took the guards and the barrier down. In hindsight,
calling the lightning might not have been the best idea. It was too
dramatic. Too obvious. She sensed that Helen was waiting for more
from her, but it was better for everyone if she kept her little secret to
herself.

"So, what brings you out to the Sunset?"

"My friend's nephew is missing. I'm trying to find him." She pulled
out the picture of Jorge and showed it to Helen.

The woman shook her head and squinted at Val. "Sorry, I don't
know him. Are you a detective or something?"

"Uh…" Her first instinct was to say no, but she could feel the sharp
outline of Malcolm's business cards in her jacket pocket. She also knew
he'd scold her if she passed up an opportunity to hand one of them

out. She swallowed and pulled out a card. "An amateur detective, maybe. I'm still getting my feet wet."

Helen frowned at the silver ink.

"Strange Activities Specialist? What does that mean?"

Val suppressed a sigh. She already regretted handing over the card.

"It means I deal with weird shit."

"What kind of weird shit? Ghosts?"

"Sometimes. Among other things."

"Like what?"

"Let's just leave it at 'weird shit.'"

They rode in silence for a few more minutes.

"That shit that happened back at the toll booth was pretty weird," Helen said.

"Yeah, it was." Val kept her tone light. She could feel Helen's eyes weighing her again.

"Any idea what caused it?"

Val shrugged. "I'm not a meteorologist. In my experience, the weather is even more mysterious than ghosts."

Helen laughed. "You're not wrong there."

Despite the misty rain, seagulls whirled overhead, crying and swooping down to snap up scraps of food. Settler's homes still crowded the edges of the freeway, but the area left open for carts had widened to two lanes, and they clattered along more easily. Val marveled at the people going about their daily business. Despite its weird placement on the reclaimed freeway, this seemed to be a normal, functioning community.

"Why did you need to go into the city, anyway?" Val asked. "I hear the Sunset is pretty self-sufficient."

"It is. But the Mission isn't. I drive into the city once a week to trade my honey at the farmer's market."

"You keep bees? Don't they sting you?"

"Not if you know how to handle them." A small smile flickered over Helen's face. Val got the feeling there was more to the story.

"So if you go into the city every week, why didn't you have money for the toll?"

Helen grimaced.

"I was mugged leaving the market. They took all my cash."

"I'm sorry."

"It happens sometimes." The woman shrugged. "I usually carry an emergency stash hidden away for the toll, but this past week some unexpected expenses came up and I had to clean out my stash. It was just bad timing."

Val scowled, remembering the way Helen had been heading into the shack to pay the toll with her body. Helen didn't seem particularly upset about it now. Maybe this wasn't the first time it had happened. Val, however, was still furious. She had let those guards off easy. She should have fried them with lightning bolts too.

Why did it always come down to sex with men? Did their daily ambition begin and end with sticking their dicks into things?

Some women knew how to make that work for them, of course. She'd seen it often enough when she was tending bar at the Alley Cat. The girls there used their sex appeal like master conductors, playing the guys who watched them dance as if they were cheap instruments. Maybe that was what they actually were.

She knew she was being unfair. There were plenty of decent guys out there. Alain. Junior. Gunter. Malcolm. The list went on. She shouldn't make demeaning generalizations. But some men were just asking for it.

As they neared Lake Merced, they passed a cluster of crumbling office buildings. The broken windows peered at them emptily.

"I guess there's not much call for office space these days," Val observed.

Helen laughed.

"Definitely not. I know a couple of buildings that have been repurposed into urban farms, but most of them are just abandoned shells."

Helen pulled the cart to a halt at the edge of the park. The green space was lush and overgrown, looking more like a wild forest than the neat urban retreat it once was.

Val hopped down from the cart.

"Thanks for the ride."

"No problem," Helen replied. "Thank you."

"For what?"

"You know, the bridge."

Val kept her expression neutral. "I'm not sure what you mean."

Helen snorted. "Whatever, Val Keri."

As the beekeeper snapped the reins over her mules, Val looked around, getting her bearings. According to the information Rosa had given her, Jorge's sister lived on the north side of the lake. Val stepped into the undergrowth, following a narrow path that headed in that general direction.

She hadn't gone more than a dozen steps before the hairs on the back of her neck prickled. She slowed but didn't stop, suddenly alert. Val scanned the area around her, trying to be cautious without letting her unseen stalker know that she was aware of being watched.

There. About thirty yards ahead and to the left. Baleful yellow eyes were watching her between the leaves.

She barely had time to register the slitted pupils before a lion burst from the undergrowth.

## 19

The lion roared, exposing teeth as long as Val's fingers. The creature's head was huge, and it appeared even bigger with the massive mane surrounding it. Thick muscles bunched and moved beneath its tawny coat. Paws the size of frisbees flexed, exposing long, curving claws.

She took a step back, hands up, every muscle in her body thrumming like struck piano wire.

"Nice kitty." She was proud her voice didn't shake. Much.

Lions were a lot bigger in person. Especially when you met them in the middle of a park with no cage between them and you. Val had always thought lions were roughly the size of a dog, but the bundle of snarling fur and muscle facing her was closer to the size of the mules that pulled Helen's cart. Bigger than any cat had a right to be.

The lion regarded her balefully, a low rumble in its throat, poised to spring. Why was a lion prowling Lake Merced? She didn't want to hurt the creature. More importantly, she didn't want the lion to hurt her.

Val took another step back … and froze as a second set of shining eyes appeared in the underbrush to her right. Then a third to her left.

She was surrounded. Not just one lion. A whole pride of lions.

"This is not good," she muttered.

*"You aren't lion,"* Mister E replied.

Val grimaced. Only the need to keep her eyes fixed on the killing machines stalking her kept her from rolling them.

"Do you have anything to add besides terrible puns?"

*"Have some pride. At least they're not dandy lions."*

Not for the first time, Val wished she could strangle the demon-cat.

She heard movement behind her and half turned to find another big cat blocking her retreat. She wondered how fast they were. Could she jump straight up and fly out of reach faster than they could pounce? Eyeing the rippling muscle beneath the sleek fur, she doubted it. If lions had anything like the speed of house cats, they would be on her before her feet left the ground.

A rough voice came from the underbrush to her left.

"Why are you trespassing on our territory?"

Confusion and hope flooded through her. Were these shifter lions? Maybe they could be reasoned with.

"I didn't know this was your territory. I'm looking for someone."

"Ignorance is no excuse," the voice hissed. "Our territory is clearly marked."

She turned toward the voice, though she still couldn't see the speaker clearly, only a shadowy silhouette moving through the underbrush. "My apologies. I was dropped off here. I don't want any trouble."

"Yet you have found trouble."

The figure stepped out and stood beside the first lion. It was short and squat, the top of its hooded head barely higher than the lion's back. In the dim light, its shape looked feminine, its squat body wrapped in layers of tattered cloth. Red eyes glinted above the scarf obscuring the bottom half of its face, while what little Val could see of its skin had a gray tint to it.

"Humans have been encroaching on our territory too much lately. Tell me why we shouldn't just kill you and leave your body as a warning to others."

Val's stomach sank. Goblins. The little scavengers were famously hostile to outsiders and extremely territorial. She had to step carefully here.

"Look, this is all a misunderstanding. I'm not familiar with the area, and I had no idea this was your territory. I got a ride down the freeway and this is where I was dropped off. I'm only here trying to find someone." She held up the picture of Jorge. "Let me walk away and no one has to get hurt."

"No one has to get hurt?" the goblin echoed, her voice thick with contempt. "The only one getting hurt here is you, intruder."

"That's debatable," Val shot back. "You and your pets might outnumber me, but I've got claws too." Her eyes shone as clouds thickened and swirled over her head. Lightning flickered. "I don't want trouble, but I won't be easy prey either."

The hackles rose on the big lion facing her. His lips peeled back in a snarl, shoulder muscles rippling as he crouched low, ready to pounce.

The goblin hissed, "A witch."

"Who are you looking for, witch?" Another squat figure emerged from the undergrowth, stepping between Val and the hostile female. Beneath the bulky layers, Val thought this one's body shape looked male. "Let us learn that before we judge this intruder."

"That is immaterial," the female snapped. "First she trespasses and now she threatens us."

"It's not a threat, it's a promise," Val said. "If you attack me, things will get ugly."

"You see? A clear threat!"

"Let me see who it is you seek." The male beckoned for the picture.

Val slowly handed it over, keeping one eye on the bristling lions. The goblin examined the picture, then showed it to the female. She cocked her head when she saw it, eyes narrowing.

"It is as I said," she spat. "She does not trespass accidentally. Her presence here is an insult."

"Perhaps." The male slid the picture into his pocket.

"Hey, that's not yours," Val snapped. "Give it back."

"Come," he turned his back on her and started to walk away. "The Goblin Queen will have questions for you."

# 20

The goblins led Val along a winding path into the heart of the old zoo. The grass had grown knee-high in the enclosures, which looked like they had survived the Collapse remarkably intact. A giraffe flicked its long purple tongue at them as they passed. Monkeys and brightly colored birds chittered in the trees overhead. Val wrinkled her nose. It smelled … well, it smelled like a zoo. One that hadn't been cleaned out in months.

"A whole city full of abandoned houses and the goblins live in the zoo?" she muttered under her breath.

"*I don't know why you find that surprising,*" Mister E replied. "*Where did you think the lions came from?*"

"Why wouldn't they prefer a house or an apartment building?"

"*Have you seen the state of the houses in this city? Ninety percent of them would fall down if you breathed on them too heavily. The zoo looks like it survived better than most neighborhoods.*"

"I suppose that's true, but still. Aren't goblins supposed to like excitement?"

"*Well, they are living with lions. I imagine that's fairly exciting. But not even the biggest thrill seekers enjoy wondering whether your bedroom ceiling is going to collapse on your head while you're sleeping. That's not thrill seek-ing, that's just stupidity."*

"Touché."

They followed the goblins into a small complex of buildings. The front doors had been smashed in, and Val stepped carefully over tooth-like shards of broken glass in the entryway. A few of the lions wandered away as they moved down a hallway with many doors on both sides, most of which had either been removed or hung on crooked hinges.

"What do you figure this was? An old administration building? A visitors' center?" Val muttered. "I wonder what they've got against doors?"

"Do you always talk about others as if they aren't there?" the female goblin snapped.

Val flinched. Apparently goblins had sharp ears.

"Only when I don't care if they can hear me," she shot back. It wasn't technically true, but she wasn't going to roll over and expose her belly to the woman. If the goblin wanted to be hostile, she was more than happy to meet her halfway.

On the other hand, she wasn't above a little passive aggressiveness either. Val smiled sweetly.

"So, are you going to answer the question then?"

"What question?"

"What do you have against doors?"

The female turned her back and stalked away. It was the male who answered.

"A tribe lives together. We have no need of doors."

Val's forehead creased. "That makes no sense. I live with house-mates, but we still have doors."

"All space belongs to the tribe. Separation makes the unit weak. Doors make the tribe weak."

"So you don't have any personal space?"

"No," he scoffed. "Goblins are not so foolish as to weaken ourselves in this way."

Val shuddered. That sounded like a special version of hell to her.

Clearly there was a lot more separating goblins from humans than simply their height and skin color.

Finally, the hall dumped them into an atrium that looked out over an enclosure of dusty yellow hills. Artificial caves had been hollowed out of the hills like eye sockets, and dozens of lions sprawled inside the sheltered spaces. Goblins sprawled among them, their bright fabrics dotting the scene like watercolor drops.

Closer, more goblins clustered among the enormous plants that had overgrown inside the atrium, exploding their pots in search of more soil, disgorging questing knots of gnarled roots. The air was redolent with the rich smells of damp soil and decay. A pair of towering palms brushed their crowns against enormous skylights high above.

In the center of the atrium, a throne of sorts had been formed out of living branches. Or perhaps they were roots; Val wasn't sure. Whatever they were, they had been braided together and shaped as they grew, and now a seat that would rival any throne dominated the space.

On the living throne lounged a short woman who looked nothing like a queen. In fact, she wouldn't have looked out of place in Alice's homeless camp beneath the Golden Gate Bridge. She wore soft brown boots and layers of bright-colored clothing that were little better than rags. Jangly beads hung upon the matted strands of hair creeping out from beneath the three hats on her head, one balanced atop the other. A large female lion lay with her head in the Goblin Queen's lap, and the colorful little woman was scratching the lion behind her ears. A deep chainsaw rumbling filled the air. With a start, Val realized the lion was purring.

When the queen noticed Val, she sprang from her throne and crossed the atrium with quick strides. Apparently, goblins did not stand on ceremony. The abandoned lion gave an indignant roar.

"A visitor!" the queen exclaimed. "Who have you brought me?"

"Not a visitor, a trespasser," the female goblin snapped. "She doesn't belong here."

"Not a trespasser," the man contradicted, "A guest."

The two goblins glared at one another so fiercely Val thought they would come to blows right there. The queen paid them no mind, circling Val and examining her curiously from every angle.

"A disagreement!" she crowed, before turning to address Val directly. She peered at the witch with close set, particolored eyes that were rounder than a humans would be. "We must get to the truth of the matter. Which is it, hmmm? Are you a trespasser or a guest?"

Val sucked in a breath, choosing her words carefully. She had no idea what constituted good manners amongst goblins, and she didn't want to start off by offending them if she could help it. Or at least — she shot a glance at the hostile female who had escorted her in — she didn't want to offend them any more than she already had.

"It was not my intention to be a trespasser, but neither is it my place to name myself a guest," she began. "As far as I know, guest rights may only be bestowed by the host. Though I would be happy to be considered as such, if you would have me."

A heavy silence followed her words. The Goblin Queen's eyes narrowed and her lips drew down into a thoughtful frown. Val braced herself for whatever explosion was clearly coming.

Then the queen laughed.

"Such fancy words! Do you think you're in the Courts of the Fae, where silver tongues paint paths with words so bright they blind you of their meaning?" The Goblin Queen hocked up a fat gob of phlegm onto the tiled atrium floor, demonstrating clearly what she thought of that.

Val was caught off balance. "I'm sorry, I thought…"

"You thought. That is your problem right there. Too much thinking. The world could do with a lot less thinking and more doing, is what I say." She bared stained and yellow teeth at Val in something that wasn't quite a smile, her eyes sparkling with challenge. "Now, tell us plainly or don't tell us at all: What are you?"

Val's chin rose to meet the inquiry. The male goblin had seemed impressed when she called the clouds. If directness was what the little woman wanted, Val would give her more than she'd bargained for.

She looked the Goblin Queen dead in the eye.

"I'm a witch."

# 21

The Goblin Queen's eyes narrowed and a crafty look stole over her face. She laughed, exposing blocky teeth.

"A witch! Do you mean you are a fortune teller? A reader of cards and lines upon a hand?"

"No," Val said flatly. "I mean a witch."

The queen's smile vanished.

"I will warn you only once. Do not claim powers you do not have. A charlatan declaring herself a witch is no laughing matter."

Val held the little woman's gaze.

"I'm not a charlatan. And I never say things I don't mean."

"Show us then." The Goblin Queen swept her hand around, including the entire atrium. "Let us see your magic."

Val folded her arms across her chest.

"I don't do party tricks."

"That is good. Because tricks will not save you if you are lying."

The queen whistled, and a pair of goblins leapt to their feet, brandishing spears. They were joined by a pair of lions. All four began to circle Val menacingly.

Val bared her own teeth.

"You don't want to do this. Your people could get hurt."

"Oh ho! My people could get hurt! The witch speaks big words." The Goblin Queen laughed as she climbed back onto her living throne. "Someone bring me some popcorn. I want to enjoy the show."

Drawing in her power, Val turned in a slow circle with the lions, trying to keep her eyes on all four of her antagonists. It was impossible. The goblins and lions spread out, encircling her completely, all the while staying in motion so she never knew exactly where each was at any given moment.

"*Yawn.*" Mister E suited deed to word. "*Stop being so defensive and attack already. You can end this before it starts.*"

"I don't want to start any trouble," Val muttered.

"*Start any trouble? Goblins and lions are stalking you. The trouble has already started. You should finish it before you get hurt.*"

"Easy for you to say."

A line of fire ripped through the back of her calf, and she whirled to find a lion bounding away from her, claws red with her blood.

"*I told you so,*" the demon-cat said smugly.

A second later something stabbed the back of her shoulder and she whirled again. This time it was the tip of a goblin's spear that was dipped in red.

"*This is embarrassing. Wake me when it's over.*"

Val snarled and punched a fist of wind out at the goblin that had stabbed her. At least, she tried to. As she gathered her power, the other lion slashed forward and pain ripped across the back of her leg once again. The attack caused her to flinch as she released her power, and the punch went wide, missing her intended target.

She whirled and unleashed a punch at the lion, only to have the goblin's spear stab forward, causing her attack to miss again.

Hot fury surged through Val. Her lips peeled back in a snarl. They were toying with her. Treating her like a plaything. She would show them the error of their ways.

As the next lion sprang forward, she spun up a whirlwind instead of a punch, cocooning herself inside a barrier of air. The big cat hit the barrier mid-leap and was knocked sprawling, claws swiping at empty space. Guttural curses filled her ears as the same thing happened to one of the goblins.

The air pressure in the atrium dropped. Black clouds gathered in the sky above, swirling and churning. Her scalp prickled, hair standing on end as Val gathered her pain and fury. Electric sparks flickered in her eyes.

Lightning bolts lanced down from the clouds. One, two, three, then more, branching and multiplying, forking out in a blinding array. Glass exploded. The ground trembled as deafening thunder shook the atrium.

When the lightning finally died away, the world had been reduced to a red smear over her flash-blinded retinas. She heard only a high-pitched squealing. The reek of ozone and burnt fur filled her nostrils.

Slowly, the atrium came back into focus.

The skylights had been destroyed. Glass shards glittered in the greenery like shards of ice. Misty rain drifted down into the atrium, speckling the broad leaves of the plants, cool against her hot cheeks.

The floor around her was scorched in a perfect black circle. Tiles had exploded like grenades, fragments flung to the far corners of the room, exposing the cement foundation beneath.

The goblins and lions that had been attacking her lay unmoving, bodies sprawled like cut flowers. Val winced. She might have gone a bit overboard.

Her eyes searched out the Goblin Queen, bracing for another attack. Surely the colorful woman would want revenge for what she'd done to her people.

The queen sat staring at Val from atop her throne, her eyes as wide as the ocean, mouth gaping. Her gaze moved from Val to the bodies of her fallen tribe members and back again.

Then she began to laugh.

"A witch indeed! Truly a witch worthy of the name!" She jumped up from her throne, appraising Val with wide eyes. "What is your name, witch?"

Val leaned away from the energetic little woman, caught off guard by both the abrupt shift in her mood and the utter disregard for her fallen tribespeople.

"My name is Val Keri," she replied cautiously.

"Val Keri." The Goblin Queen's smile grew even wider as she

repeated the name, relishing the shape of the words on her tongue. "A good, strong name for a good, strong witch. Well, Val Keri, what can I do for you?"

Val arched an eyebrow, her gaze flicking from broken skylights to the shattered floor, to her electrocuted attackers, and back to the broad grin of the Goblin Queen. Definitely not the response she would have expected. But when in Rome…

"I'm looking for information. A young man disappeared in this area recently. I'd be grateful for any information you can give me."

"Certainly, Val Keri. You have earned the warrior's right to ask questions. Who is this man you seek?"

Val beckoned to the male goblin who had escorted her in. He gingerly returned the photograph he had confiscated and she showed it to the Goblin Queen.

"His name is Jorge Reyes."

The Goblin Queen's smile disappeared from her face as if it had never existed.

# 22

"I don't think your new friend is happy to see you anymore." Mister E lounged on his side high above Val's head, blowing candy cigarette smoke rings across the atrium as he observed the proceedings like a small, furry judge.

"Tell me something I don't know," Val grumbled.

"Jorge Reyes. That name pollutes the air," the Goblin Queen snarled.

"So you know him?"

"He is a cockroach living on the bones of dead babies. I spit on his family for three generations."

Mister E grinned. *"I like this woman."*

Val ignored him and focused on the Goblin Queen.

"I'll take that as a yes. What can you tell me about him?"

"He is a foul stain beneath the armpit of a kitten."

Val took a second to process that one.

She tried to keep her tone reasonable: "What, exactly, is your conflict with him?"

"If this man is your 'friend,' I should kill you where you stand." The Goblin Queen gestured and more goblins stepped forward to surround Val. Half a dozen lions prowled the perimeter, yellow eyes fixed upon her.

Val set her feet in a defensive stance, gathering her power once more. Black clouds began to swirl.

"You can try," she challenged in a hard voice. "Maybe you'll have better luck the second time. Though I doubt it."

The two women stared at each other for a long minute as goblins and lions continued to gather, streaming in from the enclosure outside. Val tried to keep track of them but stopped counting after twenty. Any number of attackers beyond twenty simply belonged under the label of 'too many.'

"Jorge Reyes is not my friend. I've never even met him." Val tried being reasonable one final time. "He's gone missing. I've been hired to find him. That's all."

"Now the story changes," the Goblin Queen sneered. "Before you said he was your friend."

*"She's got a point. You did say that,"* Mister E confirmed.

"You are not helping," Val muttered under her breath. Out loud, she said, "I misspoke. I thought I could skip the explanation if I said I was looking for a friend. Clearly that was not the right choice of words."

The Goblin Queen's expression never changed. By now, quite the crowd had gathered around Val. She estimated that at this point 'too many' included as much as fifty goblins and half as many lions. Even slinging lightning, she would never be able to fry all of them before they overwhelmed her with sheer numbers. She might take many down with her, but she would still go down.

Val clenched her fists and bared her teeth, electricity tingling through her veins, skin itching with power as she prepared to go down swinging.

The Goblin Queen opened her mouth to order the attack, but before she could speak, a new voice rang out through the atrium.

"Stop this madness. Down this path lies ruin. I have seen it. The streets will run red with blood."

All eyes turned to the woman standing framed in the entranceway.

She wore a turquoise hoody with the hood drawn up against the rain. Bright eyes shone out of pits black as night.

"Rosa?" Val sucked in a breath. "What are you doing here?"

"Trying to stop a massacre." Rosa's voice was ragged, her shoulders slumped with fatigue. "If you fight each other here and now, the city will run red with blood. I have seen it."

"Another witch?" the Goblin Queen asked. "Are witches sprouting like mushrooms now?"

"I'm not a witch," Rosa protested, though her tone said she wasn't entirely certain.

"Are you also a friend of Jorge Reyes, new witch?" the queen demanded.

Rosa hesitated in the face of the Goblin Queens' hostility, her eyes flicking uncertainly to Val. Rosa looked like death walking. Her skin was sallow, her cheeks sunken and hollow, the skin on her face drawn as tight as a death mask. She looked like she hadn't slept in weeks. Wherever her visions were coming from, they were taking a terrible toll on her.

Val held her breath. Rosa's answer could doom them both.

Rosa opened her mouth to speak.

Val spoke first.

"This woman is a true seer. Look at her face. You see the terrible price she pays for her visions. Ignore her words at your peril."

The Goblin Queen's eyes narrowed, her gaze moving back and forth from Rosa to Val. Rosa, thankfully, had the good sense to stay silent.

The queen threw her hands up in a dramatic gesture and huffed. "Fine. I will let you live for now. Come closer. Sit. I will tell you the evils of this man you seek." She sat back down on her twisted throne and beckoned them.

Val let out a breath and cautiously lowered herself into one of the indicated chairs. She caught Rosa's eyes and surreptitiously motioned for her to have patience and remain silent. Her friend nodded and sank down next to her.

The Goblin Queen fixed them both with a glare.

"The big earthquake flattened this area. Many houses were

destroyed. People left and did not come back. We stayed. We rebuilt. We cared for the blocks nearby.

"Two months ago, a man came to our territory, asking questions. He claimed to represent the mayor's office. He said they wanted to help our community. My people showed him around. Answered all his questions. And did he help?"

*"I'm going to go ahead and guess the answer is no,"* Mister E inserted.

"First, this Jorge Reyes brought in developers. Men showed up at our doors with papers. Deeds. Saying that they were the owners of our buildings. Buildings that my people had lived in for years. Buildings that were ours by right of occupation. After the Collapse, everyone left. No one wanted these buildings. Only us. And now the humans thought they could simply return? Evict us from our homes with their pieces of paper? Of course, we refused. And do you know what he did next?"

The queen brandished a flyer.

"This is what he did. These flyers started appearing on every corner: San Francisco for San Franciscans. We didn't know what they meant. Until the humans started showing up in crowds. Holding signs and shouting. My people were assaulted in the streets. Right outside their own homes. Some fought back, but we are few and humans are many. Eventually, we were forced to flee. Abandon our homes. We had to come to dwell here, with the animals, where no humans thought to live."

The Goblin Queen looked straight at Val, her particolored eyes hard and glittering like gems. She spat onto the stone at Val's feet.

"This is what Jorge Reyes has done."

# 23

"Is it true that your nephew is a racist?" Val asked.

She and Rosa were following a goblin guide down an abandoned street, heading away from the zoo. Collapsed houses filled the neighborhood around them, piles of rubble where people had once built their lives. The briny coastal wind was chilly this close to the water and she had her hands buried in the pockets of her leather jacket, collar turned up. The little gray man tasked with leading them stayed several feet ahead and seemed determined to ignore their existence. Which suited Val just fine.

"He was a lawyer," Rosa said. "A man who loved the law. He could be seen as many things, depending on who was doing the observing."

"He loved the law? Isn't that laying it on a little thick?"

Rosa's tired mouth pressed into a sad smile.

"Not in Jorge's case, no, I don't think so. He really believed in the law. He thought it could make the world a better place. Jorge once told me that laws were the only things protecting us from ourselves. That without laws the world would be swallowed by chaos. Destroyed by endless fighting."

"That's a pretty bleak view of humanity. There are plenty of good people out there. People help each other all the time without being forced to by the law."

"Sure, but is he really wrong? Look around you. For every good person there's some might-makes-right asshole throwing his weight around, trying to take a bigger slice of the pie. Laws are the only thing that keeps them in check."

"Enforcement of the law keeps them in check," Val corrected. "People like that will bend or break the rules every chance they get. If nobody holds them accountable, laws are meaningless."

"Exactly. Without laws, what standard do you have to hold them accountable to?"

Val pondered that for a moment.

"Basic morality standards?"

"Yes, but moral standards vary wildly. What one person finds perfectly acceptable, another may find abhorrent. The law is the final arbiter of morality."

"You sound like you've thought about this a lot."

Rosa chuckled, the sound dry and hollow in her chest.

"Jorge thought about it a lot. I'm just repeating what he said to me."

"So you don't actually believe what you're saying?"

"No, I believe it. You would too, if you talked to him long enough. He makes some pretty convincing arguments."

They lapsed into silence as Val considered Rosa's words. Her eyes roamed over the collapsed houses as they passed. Where Val lived, in the Mission, there was still a lot of structural damage from the big quake, but most of it was minor stuff easy to overlook. Small cracks in the walls or asphalt. An occasional telephone pole that had fallen on a parked car and never been removed. Things that people could work around and still get on with their lives.

Not here. The neighborhood around them had been flattened, leaving most of the houses little more than piles of brick and broken cinder blocks. Collapsed walls and destroyed lives. Val saw pieces of furniture and clothing torn and broken. Children's toys half buried in the dust. Rusted shells of cars that would never move again.

"The law didn't help these people much," she found herself saying.

Rosa followed her gaze, her eyes sad.

"No, it didn't. Some things are bigger than the law. Nature doesn't care about our rules. She does what she wants. She's a big, bad bitch. Kind of like you."

A startled sound burst from Val.

"Easy there. I think you've got me mixed up with somebody else."

"No, really." Rosa turned earnest eyes to her. "You saved me from the fae. You fought the Harbinger of Winter and won. How many people do you think could do that? You are one bad-ass bitch, Val Keri."

Val looked at her feet and wished she was somewhere else. Her fingers strayed to her shoulder, unconsciously tracing the memento mori tattoo beneath her jacket. She didn't deserve Rosa's praise. Too many people had died on her watch. Some of them she'd killed herself. Accidentally or on purpose, it didn't matter. Dead was dead. She was no hero. Far from it.

Their goblin guide's voice pulled her from her thoughts, "We have arrived."

He pointed to a modern apartment building that covered most of a block. Shockingly, it was still standing amidst the sea of collapsed houses.

"That used to be goblin territory?" Val asked.

"We lived there for years," he snarled. "After the quake everyone tried to take it from us. We had to fight for our homes. And we did. We defended our territory against everyone."

"So what happened?"

"Lawyers," he spat. "The mayor's office sent their lawyers with papers and notices. We ignored them. They came back with the police. They evicted us from our homes so they could give them to humans instead."

"And the man we're looking for was one of the lawyers?"

"The queen said he was, didn't she? Ask apartment 101." The goblin turned his back and walked away.

Apartment 101 turned out to be around the back, at the far corner of the building. An ancient oak tree loomed over the door, dominating a tiny patch of dirt that someone nearsighted and in a generous mood might have called a yard. The door itself looked the same as all the neighboring ones, made of plain brown wood and unadorned aside from the number 101 in brass numbers. Actually, that wasn't entirely true. Below the number was also a brass knocker in the shape of a hand holding a polished ball.

Val lifted the hand to reveal a brass plate beneath it that the gripped ball would bang against when the knocker was released. She turned to Rosa and raised an eyebrow.

"Is it just me, or does this hand look like a fortune teller holding a crystal ball?"

"It's not just you."

Val frowned. "It seems out of place in this modern building. I don't like it."

"It does seem a little on the nose," Rosa agreed. "On the other hand, what else are we going to do?"

"I see what you did there," Val said. "And I don't like that either." So saying, she released the hand, letting it swing down and bang the metal ball against the door.

The brass-on-brass made a surprisingly loud sound, reverberating through the heavy wood for extra volume. Val and Rosa both jumped, then giggled nervously.

The sound lingered in the air for several seconds before slowly dying away. They heard no response from within the apartment. After standing there for nearly a minute, Val looked at Rosa.

"Why don't you knock this time. Maybe you'll have better luck."

Rosa shrugged and reached for the hand. No sooner had her fingers touched the brass than the door was flung open.

A willowy old woman in a bright pink tracksuit proclaimed, "Have some patience! Can't a body take a shit in peace?"

## 24

"Um," Val stammered. "Sorry about that."

"What do you want?" The woman in the tracksuit eyed them suspiciously. Her nails were flawless french tips, her pure white hair immaculately cut just above her shoulders.

Val looked at Rosa, but Rosa was looking at her. Oh, right. She was the professional here.

"Hi, I'm looking into a missing person's case and I was wondering if I could ask you a few questions."

The old woman raised an eyebrow. "Missing persons?"

"My nephew," Rosa rasped. "He's missing."

The woman looked from Val to Rosa and back again. She pursed her lips in suspicion.

"Please," Rosa added.

The exhaustion and desperation in Rosa's voice combined with the 'please' seemed to do the trick. The willowy woman wavered, then stood aside.

"I suppose you'd better come in."

They followed the woman into a shockingly modern apartment. It smelled of fresh vanilla extract. Val was surprised to find the woman's furniture was all sparse, clean lines. Cream colored leather couches stood beside marble-topped end tables. A crystal vase containing exactly three flowers was the only decoration atop a matching polished dining table flanked by severe, straight-backed chairs. Val found it surprising because sparse modernism was not a style she generally associated with old people. Old people's homes were cluttered with mementos of the past and furnishings thirty years out of fashion. Not this woman's. Her apartment was so sharply modern, it almost hurt to look at.

"Sit." The woman motioned to the uncomfortable-looking chairs, then turned and disappeared into the kitchen without waiting to see if her command would be obeyed.

Val and Rosa shrugged at each other and did as they were bid.

A few minutes later, the woman returned with a silver tray and the rich aroma of fresh coffee. She placed china cups with saucers in front of Val and Rosa, and one for herself in front of an empty chair across from them. A sweating pitcher of milk, tiny bowl of sugar, and a plate of ginger cookies all went in the center of the table, beside the flowers.

"Which one of you knocked on my door?" the woman asked without preamble the instant her butt was settled in a chair.

"That would be me," Val admitted sheepishly. "Sorry, it was louder than I thought it would be."

"Interesting." The woman assessed her as she stirred cream into her coffee. Her irises were the hazel of a field of wheat in summer. Val realized with a start that they were almost as gold as her own.

When the woman didn't say anything else, Val ventured, "So, about our missing person…"

"Are you both witches, or is it just you?" The woman interrupted. She continued before either of them had a chance to answer. "I think it must be both of you. How fascinating."

Val's mouth opened and closed but no sound came out. Rosa jumped in to fill the awkward silence.

"How did you know that?"

"I have my ways," the woman said mysteriously. Then she added with a wink, "But I'll give you this one for free. It's the door knocker. It reads anyone who touches it. It's quite handy for avoiding unwanted guests."

Val's mind reeled. This woman, with her ultra-modern furnishings and pink tracksuit, was a witch? How was that possible? She had never met a witch that didn't look the part. This woman looked like she had a closet full of power suits and a lifetime membership to LA Fitness.

"What, you don't think I look like a witch?" The woman smirked and Val flinched, wondering if she was reading her mind somehow. "So, how did you find me? I've got this place warded tighter than Baryshnikov's dance belt. I have to admit, I'm impressed you tracked me down."

"Actually, we didn't," Val admitted. "A goblin told us to talk to you."

The old woman laughed. "Well, that's reassuring. For a minute there I thought I'd lost a step." Abruptly, she held out a hand. "I'm Giselle."

*"Giselle?"* Mister E asked. *"Is she by chance a retired supermodel? It would explain the decor."*

Giselle cocked her head as if she heard a mosquito buzzing around her ear. Val hurried to distract her, clasping the old witch's hand in hers.

"Val Keri. And this is Rosa Reyes."

The old woman didn't let go of Val's hand, but instead took Rosa's hand in her other, holding them both so they remained connected in an odd triangle surrounding the three flowers. Val noticed the blooms were all different: a red rose, a yellow daisy, and a purple orchid. The old woman's skin was parchment thin, but her grip was strong, despite the bones and tendons clearly standing out on the back of her hands. Val tried to disengage, but Giselle would not release her. She could feel power flowing across the connection like an open tap, running through her to Giselle and Rosa and back again.

Giselle's hazel eyes held Val's before moving deliberately to Rosa's and then back again.

"Now. Tell me why you're here."

"We're looking for Rosa's nephew," Val said, holding up Jorge's picture with her other hand. "We were hoping you might have seen him."

But she already knew that Giselle recognized Jorge. The old woman tried to keep a poker face, but the faint tightening of her grip gave her away. Still, the old woman wasn't ready to concede the game just yet.

"Why would you think I might know anything about it?" she said, still clasping their hands and holding their gazes.

"Because the goblin told us to talk to you," Val said.

Before Giselle could reply, Rosa added, "And because I know it to be true."

The old woman looked ready to protest, then she sighed and released their hands.

"You are a seer," she said to Rosa.

It wasn't a question, but Rosa inclined her head anyway.

"I guess maybe I am. I don't know. It's all kind of new to me."

"And confusing," Giselle said.

"And confusing," Rosa agreed.

The old woman's eyes turned to Val.

"But your powers are not new."

Again it wasn't a question, so Val simply said, "Neither are yours."

Giselle's lips turned up at the corners.

"No, they are not." She stirred milk into her coffee and took a deliberate bite of ginger cookie. Only after washing it down with a sip of coffee did she fold her hands on top of the table and say, "OK, fine. I'll agree to an exchange of information. Question for question. What would you like to know?"

# 25

"Do you know Jorge Reyes?" Val asked.

"Yes," Giselle replied simply. Before Val could ask for clarification, Giselle turned her gaze on Rosa and said, "How long have you been having visions?"

"Um, a couple of months?" Rosa said. "But they've gotten really bad the last couple of weeks."

"Every night?" Giselle asked.

Rosa opened her mouth to speak, but Val stopped her with a chopping hand gesture.

"Our turn. Question for question. When was the last time you saw Jorge Reyes?"

The corners of Giselle's mouth curled up again. She inclined her head toward Val.

"I see you've played this game before."

"I catch on fast. When was the last time you saw Jorge Reyes?"

Giselle steepled her fingers in front of her.

"It must have been what, two weeks ago?" She fixed her gaze of Rosa. "Wouldn't you say?"

Rosa's mouth dropped open.

"Are you saying my visions are connected to Jorge's disappearance?"

Giselle lifted a shoulder clad in pink fabric. Let it fall.

"It seems pretty obvious to me."

"But why…"

"Ah, ah. My turn." Giselle turned her gaze to Val. "Are you the witch that took out the vampire coven?"

"I had help," Val said.

"I should hope so. Otherwise I wouldn't want to be anywhere within a city block of you. Anyone who can take out an entire vampire coven alone is someone you would do well to steer clear of."

"Noted."

"Why would my visions get worse when Jorge disappeared?" Rosa asked.

"As they say, blood is thicker than water, darling. What is he to you? Your brother?"

"My nephew," Rosa admitted. "But he's like a son to me. I helped my sister raise him."

"There's your answer," Giselle said. "Your connection to him is stronger than simple blood. Maternal connections are extremely powerful. No wonder you sensed when he disappeared."

"Where did you last see Jorge?" Val asked.

"I didn't get my question," Giselle protested.

"Yes, you did. You asked Rosa what Jorge is to her."

Giselle made a face. "A technicality, but I'll allow it."

Val opened her mouth to ask again, but Giselle halted her with a raised palm.

"I'm getting to your question. Let an old lady breathe a moment."

Val fidgeted while Giselle took another bite of ginger cookie and washed it down with a sip of coffee. Val impatiently sipped her own coffee while waiting. The flavor was as fine as Giselle's furnishings, rich and nutty. All that was missing was a splash of butterscotch, and it would be perfect.

*"It probably came out of a civet's asshole,"* Mister E said.

Val choked and barely managed to not spit her coffee across the table. Giselle watched her coughing and eye-watering with a frown. Finally, Val got herself under control.

"Sorry about that," she croaked. "I believe you were about to tell us when you saw Jorge Reyes last."

Giselle rolled her eyes. "Fine, I'll tell you the story. I'm getting tired of this game anyway. You came from the goblins, so I assume you've already heard their version of it?"

"We heard that Jorge helped Mayor Light get the goblins evicted from this building."

The older woman's silver head waggled back and forth. "That's a bit reductive, but close enough. I've been living here the whole time, which is why I assume the goblins sent you to me."

"Why didn't you get evicted too?"

Giselle snorted. "Do I look like a goblin to you? I've been here a long time and my wards are airtight. Nobody gets into this apartment that I don't want in here. That includes lawyers with eviction notices."

"But you let them evict the goblins." There was accusation in Val's tone.

"Honey, look at this apartment. Does it look like I run a charity? My services are not cheap. Those goblins couldn't afford me. Also, they didn't ask. Goblins are too proud and independent. So don't take that judgmental tone with me; they wouldn't ask for outside help if their lives depended on it."

Val didn't like it, but she gave Giselle a small nod, acknowledging the point.

"Anyway, Jorge Reyes helped Mayor Light evict the goblins. And a bunch of the mayor's people took their place."

"The mayor's people? Like his staff?" Val asked.

"A few. But mostly I think the mayor wanted some people to be indebted to him."

"Why did the mayor evict the goblins? And what does this have to do with Jorge's disappearance?" Rosa leaned forward impatiently.

"I'm getting to that. Don't get your panties in a bunch." Out of spite, Giselle paused for another cookie and coffee break.

The moment Giselle's lips touched the rim of her mug, Mister E whispered in Val's ear, *"Poop beans."*

She was ready for it this time and managed to stifle her laugh by pressing her lips into a tight line. Rosa scowled but said nothing.

Giselle leaned back in her chair and fixed them with her golden eyes.

"To begin with, you're asking the wrong questions. You're focusing on the goblins, when you should be focusing on the building."

Val cocked her head.

"Wait, are you saying that the evictions weren't targeting the goblins for being goblins? They were about the building in some way?"

"Exactly."

"But why?"

"Well, you know what they say." Giselle smiled. "Location, location, location."

## 26

"So the eviction wasn't racially motivated?" Val asked.

"It's easy to assume that it was, isn't it?" Giselle replied. "Almost too easy."

Val's eyes widened.

"That's what Mayor Light wants us to assume."

Wheels turned in Val's mind as she tried to fit this new information into the puzzle.

"He's a man who loudly and forcefully denounces magical creatures every chance he gets. Of course everyone would think he hates goblins. But if you're saying all that is just a smokescreen..." Val frowned. "Except that's not true. I was there when his followers attacked the Mission Shifter Settlement. The mayor gave a speech and whipped them into a frenzy. He was directly responsible for the violence. I saw it with my own eyes."

"I'm not saying he's not a racist. In all probability, he is. What I'm saying is that he uses that racism to draw attention away from his real goals," Giselle clarified.

"Pay no attention to the man behind the curtain."

"Exactly."

Val swore.

"It was bad enough when I thought he was a racist demagogue. But if he's cynically stoking people's fear and hatred to mask his real goals, that makes him a hundred times worse."

"I don't understand." Rosa looked from Val to Giselle, her forehead furrowed in confusion. "What does this have to do with Jorge?"

"Jorge was working for Mayor Light. Doing his dirty work."

"No, he wouldn't do that. He's a good person."

"You told me yourself that Jorge believed in the law, right? Which means that as long as Light was operating within the strict confines of the law, he wouldn't have a problem with the mayor's policies. No matter how immoral or hateful they might appear to us." Val spoke quickly as facts clicked into place. "What if he didn't know that Light's bluster was all a facade? What if he discovered the mayor's real endgame, and it turned out to be against the law? What if he refused to go along with it?"

Rosa sucked in a breath. "Jorge realized what he was doing was wrong. He was going to expose the mayor's plan."

Val wanted to point out that, technically, racism was also wrong and that by most moral standards everything her nephew had done in service to a man like Mayor Light could be considered wrong. But she kept her silence. She knew her friend was hurting, and that she loved her nephew, was worried about him and wanted to think the best of him.

Giselle spoke before Val could figure out a way to articulate any of this.

"I know you want to believe the best of your nephew, but there's a simpler, more human explanation."

"Extortion," Val agreed. "Jorge demanded payment in exchange for his silence."

*"I believe lawyers call that a retainer fee,"* Mister E said. *"In this case, it would have been to retain his loyalty. Money talks. Or in this case, doesn't talk."*

Rosa covered her mouth with her hand. "Oh no. No no no."

Val watched her friend age as the realization hit her, the shadowed hollows on her face deepening with every 'no.' She wanted to comfort

Rosa. Reassure her that everything was going to be all right. But the only comfort she could offer was the cold comfort of facts.

"It's still only a theory," she said. "All we're doing is tossing out ideas. It's part of the process. We don't actually know anything yet. Don't jump to conclusions until we uncover concrete evidence."

"But how do we do that?" Rosa latched on to Val's words like a drowning woman clutching a chunk of driftwood. "Where's the evidence?"

"That's what we're going to find out," Val assured her. She turned back to Giselle. "Do you have any evidence? Or is this all some crazy conspiracy theory that won't survive Occam's Razor?"

Giselle glanced at Rosa before she spoke. Regret colored her words.

"I saw your nephew arguing with the mayor in front of the building one day. I wasn't close enough to hear what he was saying, but he was waving his arms around and screaming at Mayor Light."

"What did the mayor do?" Rosa shrank in her seat, eyes wide with fear.

"Nothing at the time. He didn't say a word. He just stood there while Jorge got all red in the face and ranted at him. But Light got this really cold, disdainful look on his face. As if your nephew was some disgusting thing stuck to the bottom of his shoe that needed to be scraped off. As if he had crossed some line that couldn't be uncrossed and Light was done with him."

"Then what happened?"

"Nothing happened. Your nephew stormed off down the street and Light got back into his limo and left."

"When was the next time you saw Jorge?" Val asked.

"I didn't. I never saw him again."

"Why didn't you call the police?" Rosa demanded.

"Why would I?" Giselle shrugged. "I assumed he'd been sacked after his outburst. I didn't think any more about it until you showed up looking for him."

"How long ago was this?" Val had to ask, although she felt sure she already knew the answer.

"A couple of weeks ago."

"Which matches the timeline of when Jorge went missing."

"And that's when my dreams started getting worse." Rosa clutched at Val's arm. "What do we do?"

Val fought the urge to yank her sleeve from Rosa's grip.

"We work the case," she said firmly. "All we have are half-baked theories. We need to stick to the facts.

"Fact one: Jorge was working for Mayor Light and helped to get the goblins evicted from this building.

"Fact Two: Jorge was seen screaming at Mayor Light a few weeks ago.

"Fact Three: Rosa's prophetic dreams started getting worse around that time.

"Fact Four: Jorge has not been seen since then. At least not by anybody in this room. Am I leaving anything out?"

She caught Giselle's and Rosa's eyes in turn. When neither of them spoke, she continued, "So our mission statement remains unchanged. We still haven't found Jorge. We keep working the case until we do."

Rosa nodded, her lips pressed into a worried line. She still looked exhausted and frightened, but Val's calm recitation of the facts seemed to have reassured her a little.

"So what's our next step?" Rosa asked in a tight voice. She was trying very hard to keep her fear under control.

Val turned to Giselle. "Is there anything else you can tell us?"

The older woman cocked her head, considering. Then she shook her head once, a sharp, definitive negation.

"No. I don't believe I know anything further that's relevant."

"OK." Val downed the rest of her coffee in a single gulp and stood up. "Now we dig deeper."

# 27

"Don't these people all work for Mayor Light?" Rosa gnawed on her cuticles as she trailed Val down the hall. At least two of her fingers were bleeding. "Why would any of them tell us anything?"

They were doing detective work the old-fashioned way. Knocking on doors and asking questions. They'd been working their way through the building for the past twenty minutes and had learned exactly nothing. Val feared Rosa might be correct, but they needed to do their due diligence. Besides, she wasn't exactly brimming with better ideas.

"Jorge worked for Mayor Light too," she pointed out. "Just because you work for someone, doesn't mean you agree with everything they do. Jorge must have had some friends on the staff who would be willing to talk to us. We just have to find them. Also, I don't think everyone in this building works for Light."

"Even if they don't work for him, they owe him for evicting the goblins and putting them in these apartments instead."

Val couldn't argue with Rosa there.

Although the building had been fixed up, there were still some lingering signs that it had once been home to a tribe of goblins. For one, most of the doors looked brand new. Val was fairly certain they had been installed after the goblins were evicted. As she'd learned in the zoo, goblins had little use for doors. Also, beneath the fresh paint on the walls, she could see places where strange designs, writing, and art had been carved into them. She wasn't sure why the mayor's minions had thought they could erase those things by simply slapping paint over them instead of replacing the vandalized drywall. Paint was cheaper and easier, she supposed.

Her stomach rumbled as she lifted her hand to knock on the door of the next apartment, and she cursed herself for not taking a handful of Giselle's ginger cookies with her. Not that ginger cookies would get her very far, but they'd certainly get her further than an empty stomach. Her mood was plummeting along with her blood sugar; hungry and cranky was no way to conduct an investigation.

But it had been a long journey out here to the Sunset, and she needed to turn over as many stones as she could while she was there. Better to work hungry than to have to come all the way back again tomorrow.

Also, Rosa was with her now, and Val had a feeling Rosa would pound on doors all night if she had to, whether Val was with her or not.

She eyed her friend out of the corner of her eye. Gone was the cute, confident, sassy shopkeeper who had been kidnapped and impersonated by the Harbinger of Winter. In her place was a hollow-eyed wraith.

Rosa had become painfully thin, skin stretched so tight over her skull that Val felt like she was looking at a walking skeleton. While Rosa hadn't necessarily been voluptuous, her body had possessed a healthy dose of curves. Val recalled admiring the way Rosa's ass had filled out her jeans, the thickness of her thighs.

Those same jeans now hung on Rosa's frame as if her hipbones were a wire hanger. Val was sure it couldn't only be from a lack of food and sleep. She guessed that Rosa's prophetic dreams demanded a ton of energy. Her new powers were burning her up from the inside out. Sucking her dry.

She worried there would be nothing left of her friend by the time this was over. The visions would use her up and leave her a dead, empty husk.

Fae gifts were often like that. The fae either didn't know or didn't care that the human body wasn't able to contain that much power. Maybe they found it amusing, or even got off on it. Some of the fae were exactly that type of asshole.

She wished she could help Rosa. Give the woman some of her own magic to sustain her. Somehow balance out the cruel gift that was eating her alive.

But Val's magic didn't work that way. Her power was external, not internal. If you wanted something destroyed, she was your woman.

If you needed something fixed? A friend healed?

Not so much.

She sighed, her hands curling into fists at her side, nails digging into her palms. The only way she could help was to do exactly what she was doing. Help her friend find Jorge. Rosa's dreams had intensified when Jorge disappeared. When they found him, her visions would go back to being a sporadic nuisance, instead of the constant nightmare they were now.

Hopefully.

If they didn't... Well. Val refused to let herself think too deeply about that.

She would find Jorge.

Period.

That was all there was to it.

Her knuckles rapped against the door. She cocked her head, listening for movement inside. Very few people opened the door to strangers these days. And with good reason. The city was a dangerous place. Generally, Val approved of this type of caution.

However, when she was the stranger doing the knocking, the reclusiveness quickly became very annoying.

She thought she heard some rustling on the other side of the door. No barking, so it wasn't a dog. Could be a cat, though.

The sound repeated. Was that fabric swishing? Hard to tell, exactly.

But some instinct told Val the sound wasn't made by an animal. There was a human inside. Probably trying to stay quiet and pretend they weren't home, hoping whoever was at the door would go away.

If that person thought they would be put off so easily, they had a rude awakening coming. Val was tired, she was hungry, and her friend's nephew was missing, while Rosa herself was being consumed by malignant prophetic visions.

She wasn't leaving this building without answers.

"Open up," she bellowed, knocking again. "We need to ask you some questions about a missing persons case."

Val pressed her ear to the door and waited to see if that would produce the desired result. She heard more rustling sounds, but the door still didn't open.

"I know you're in there. We won't take up much of your time. I just need to ask you a few questions."

Still nothing.

Val ground her teeth. This person was beginning to piss her off.

"We can do this the easy way, or we can do it the hard way," she called. "The easy way is you open the door, answer a few questions, and we both go on with our day. The hard way is you keep pretending you're not home and I kick in your door and you answer my questions anyway. In that scenario I am not liable for damages to either your door or your person. It's your choice. So which is it going to be?"

Rosa looked at her aghast.

"You can't just…"

Val cut her off with an abrupt gesture.

"I know that, and you know that, but they don't know that," she whispered back. "Trust me, OK? Most of the time the threat is more powerful than the action."

The rustling sounds grew closer, but the door still did not open.

"Last chance," Val called. "I'm kicking this door down on the count of three. One. Two…"

The lock clicked, and the door swung partially open. Peering out at Val uncertainly was a girl with black-coffee skin and blue hair cascading off her head in a wave.

Val recognized her instantly. Miranda. Jorge's ex-girlfriend. The girl's brow crinkled between her eyes.

"Val Keri? What are you doing here?"

## 28

"I don't know anything more than I did the last time you asked me," Miranda insisted.

The three of them were sitting in the living room of her apartment, which, while not as chic as Giselle's, definitely indicated that Miranda was doing all right for herself. The dusky light of the waning sunset slanted in through the window. Miranda's apartment was nicer than Jorge's little studio by a long shot. Which made Val extremely curious as to exactly what Miranda did for a living.

Unlike Giselle, Miranda hadn't offered them coffee or cookies after she very reluctantly allowed them to come into her apartment. Given the empty churning of Val's stomach, this felt like an extremely rude personal attack.

*"You did threaten to kick in her door."* Mister E lay sprawled across the back of the couch, his top hat perched on his head at a jaunty angle. *"You can't blame the girl if she's not particularly happy to see you."*

"She could still offer us snacks," Val grumped under her breath. "Everybody likes snacks."

To Miranda, she said, "Were you here the day Jorge got into a screaming match with Mayor Light in front of the building? Do you know what it was about?"

Miranda's eyes shifted to the side, which gave Val her answer immediately. Still, she patiently waited to see how much the girl was willing to admit.

"I'm not sure which day you're talking about," Miranda evaded.

"So there were multiple instances of Jorge screaming at his boss? That doesn't sound like a very healthy work environment."

"No ... that's not what I meant," Miranda stammered.

"What did you mean?" Val pinned the girl with her golden stare.

Miranda's eyes fluttered around the room like a moth seeking escape. But she was trapped with nowhere to hide.

Val wondered what exactly the girl was trying to hide. As someone who had presumably cared about Jorge, she'd expected Miranda to be cooperative, but so far the girl had been anything but. Val's spider sense was tingling now. She was determined to find out why.

Miranda blew out a nervous breath, her fingers busy unraveling the cuff of her sweater.

Finally, she spoke, "Jorge disagreed with some of the things the mayor said. But not ... never like that. He didn't yell at him or anything. He wasn't like that."

"So that day was unusual?"

"Yes," Miranda gratefully latched onto the line Val threw her. "It was unusual."

"Why was it unusual? What happened that day to set Jorge off?"

Miranda's expression became panicked as she realized too late the line had a hook in it.

"Please." Rosa put a hand on Miranda's arm "He's my nephew. We just want to find him."

Coming from the old Rosa, this would have been a calming and supportive gesture. But when a walking skeleton put a hand on you, it was anything but calming.

Miranda jerked her arm away. Surprise and hurt flashed across Rosa's face. She swallowed and blinked back tears. Judging by how tired Rosa looked, Val was amazed her friend wasn't constantly crying. She knew she would be. Hell, she wanted to cry right now, and she was only hungry.

"What happened that day?" Val pressed, her voice hard.

Miranda wilted.

"I don't really know the details. Jorge wouldn't tell me. Attorney-client confidentiality or something like that. All I know is that there was something Mayor Light wanted. Something they uncovered or found ... maybe a piece of property... I'm not really sure. I don't know what it was. All I know is that, whatever it was, the mayor wanted it bad. But whoever had it didn't want to give it to him. And from what I gathered, there wasn't a clear legal way for the mayor to get it."

Miranda swallowed, her eyes landing anywhere but on Val.

"The mayor ordered Jorge to get the thing for him by whatever means necessary. Even if that meant breaking the law. Jorge refused, of course. The law is his religion. He'll employ loopholes and shady tricks to achieve an objective, sure. But outright breaking the law? No way. When the mayor insisted, Jorge went ballistic. That was what the screaming match was about."

"Have you seen Jorge since then?" Val asked.

Miranda nodded. "Just once. Later that night."

*"Now we're getting somewhere."* Mister E leaned forward on the back of the couch.

"And?" Val prompted.

Miranda licked her lips.

"I don't know. He stopped by here and demanded I let him in. Kind of like you did." She shot Val a look, which Val ignored. "After I let him in, I don't know. He was ranting. He wasn't making a lot of sense. I don't really know what he was talking about. He stomped around the apartment for maybe ten minutes, spouting off about crazy things, then he left. And I haven't seen him since."

"What was he ranting about?"

"I told you, I don't..."

"Even if it doesn't make any sense. Are there any details that stuck in your mind? Anything at all you can tell us?"

"Please," Rosa added. "Any little detail could help us find him."

Miranda sighed.

"I really don't remember, but I'll try." She made a thinking face, the tip of her tongue poking out between her lips. "I think there was something about aliens? Or artifacts? Alien artifacts? Native alien artifacts?" She shook her head. "I really don't know. Like I said, he was ranting."

"You're doing fine," Val encouraged. "Were these artifacts the thing that Mayor Light wanted?"

"I think so? Maybe? I don't remember him mentioning Mayor Light. I don't know if the two things are connected at all."

"Did he tell you where the artifacts were? Who they belonged to?"

"I don't... Oh, wait!" Miranda's face lit up. "I do remember something. He said there was a dig ... uh... a foundation! They were digging a foundation!"

"Do you know where the foundation is?"

"No. I don't think he said exactly where it was. But I know it was somewhere nearby. Within a couple of blocks, I think. I know some people working on the project live in this building."

Val exchanged hopeful glances with Rosa. This sounded like a solid lead.

"Is there anything else you remember? Anything at all?"

Miranda shook her head.

"No, I'm sorry. That's all I've got."

Val stood up, excitement pumping through her veins, eager to start chasing down this new lead. Rosa followed suit.

"Thank you. You've been incredibly helpful." Val slid one of her business cards onto the coffee table. "Please let me know if you remember anything else."

Val and Rosa charged off into the deepening evening gloom.

# 29

Outside, the sky was brushed a deep ochre. Night was falling fast, and Val pulled her jacket closed. The wind had picked up as well, the ocean breeze taking on an evening chill that hadn't been present earlier.

"Where are we going?" Rosa demanded, struggling to keep up with Val's rapid strides.

"The excavation site. Those artifacts are important. I can feel it."

"But we don't even know where it is!"

"Miranda said it was close. It shouldn't be too hard to find."

"Seriously? We're in a city, Val. 'Close' could be ten blocks from here. In any direction." Rosa flung her arms wide, indicating the expanse of crumbled houses surrounding them. "That's too much ground to cover by randomly wandering around and hoping we get lucky."

"Then it's a good thing I'm not planning on randomly wandering around, isn't it?"

Val abruptly veered into the driveway of a completely flattened house. Half the garage still stood, and she ducked inside this shelter. By the time Rosa caught up to her, Val was already kicking debris off the floor, creating a spot shielded from the wind by the two walls still standing.

"What are you doing?" Rosa puffed, trying to catch her breath. She watched Val pull out a piece of chalk and start drawing lines on the part of the cement floor she had cleared.

Rosa was always tired these days. Exhausted, really. It felt like more than simply the stress of her constant worrying about Jorge or the fact that she could barely force herself to eat because food tasted like cardboard or the visions that kept her from getting a good night's sleep. There was a restless, anxious energy inside her, burning her up.

It was as if every sense she had was perpetually on high alert, looking for danger — and even some senses she didn't have. Or didn't know she had. It was confusing and hard to describe. It was like her spirit was constantly questing outward, sensing the world around her in ways that she didn't understand. It probably had something to do with the fae power she'd been infected with, and the horrible visions that accompanied it.

And the visions truly were horrible. Streets bathed in blood. People eviscerated. Crowds torn apart limb by limb.

She didn't mind the fact that she could see the future. It was kind of cool, honestly. But did the visions all have to be nightmare fuel? Why couldn't she be shown what would happen without being terrorized out of her wits?

That was assuming, of course, that the visions weren't literal. She figured that things like buckets of blood raining from the sky had to be symbolic. Because if they weren't... She shuddered. Things were going to get a *whole lot* worse.

Rosa watched as Val finished drawing a pentagram inside a circle. The witch pulled candle stubs from her pockets and placed them at the corners of the star.

She tried to calm her anxiety by telling herself that she could have faith in Val. After all, Val had rescued her from the Harbinger of Winter. Hell, Val had saved the whole city from a fae invasion. Surely finding Jorge was simpler than that. Val Keri would get to the bottom of whatever trouble he'd gotten himself into.

Her nephew was still alive. She knew he was still alive. Her visions told her he was still alive.

Sort of.

It was confusing. Something had happened to him. She was sure of that. He was definitely in some kind of trouble. Big, life-changing trouble. But she knew he wasn't dead. Hurting, but not dead. Not exactly. Rosa could take comfort in that.

She just wished the icy fear clutching her heart would get the message.

"What are you doing?" she asked as Val sat down inside the pentagram and lit the candles.

"Casting a tracking spell. I gathered some of Jorge's hair from his apartment. If he's near here, the spell will tell me in which direction to look."

A tracking spell sounded good. Useful. Hopeful. Something else to take comfort in.

Rosa's anxiety didn't lessen.

She watched as Val held a few hairs up in front of her and lit them on fire. The hair on the back of her neck prickled. She *felt* the energy from Val's spell. That was new. It was like she and Val were tuned to the same wavelength now—which was somehow both comforting and terrifying.

The burnt hairs produced a lot more smoke than Rosa had expected. It swirled around Val, thickening, always staying inside the boundaries of the circle she'd drawn. Then Val did something Rosa didn't catch, made some gesture or murmured some word, and suddenly the smoke was free, streaming out of the circle like a hound released on a hunt, baying off in pursuit of its quarry.

She felt this magical release as more than simply hairs rising on the back of her neck. Her whole body shivered as if she'd been dunked in a lake of ice. It was cold and shocking, every one of her nerves felt alive and painfully aware.

The smoke brushed past Rosa as if it were a living thing. A massive soft animal brushing against her. She turned to follow its flight as it streamed out of the garage and off into the night.

Something brushed her elbow and she turned to find Val standing beside her, the witch also peering in the direction of the fleeing smoke. Val's golden eyes were luminous in the dark and she crackled with power that Rosa could feel in her bones. Standing next to her was like standing next to a bonfire on a cold Pacific Ocean beach.

Val turned to her and scowled.

"It didn't work."

Rosa didn't understand that. She could feel the smoke out there, the power of Val's spell lurking like some massive beast. Watching her with silent, glowing eyes in the darkness.

She opened her mouth to tell Val as much... but the beast flowed into her mouth instead.

Rosa burned as Val Keri's magic filled her, crackling through her senses. Power scalded her insides, searing magma flowing through her veins.

Rosa screamed.

Darkness covered her eyes as she fell down, down, down into the bottomless depths of her vision.

# 30

Val paced the floor of the garage, watching over Rosa. Her friend twitched and moaned on the cold concrete, head thrashing from side to side. Val had balled up her jacket and put it under Rosa's head for a pillow. It was all she could think to do. There was no spell she could cast, no healing potion she could pour down her friend's throat. All she could do was stand vigil and keep her safe. So she paced, praying that whatever power had Rosa in its grip would release her soon.

Periodically, her eyes strayed to the darkness beyond the garage door. Her senses quested out into the night, searching for some trace of her tracking spell. Hoping against hope that the spell would find something and flare back to life, giving her some clue to follow.

Val wasn't a patient woman by nature. She needed to be in motion, keep moving, to always be doing something, working toward some goal.

But there was nothing here. No spell to follow. No mystic surety of purpose. Nothing to see and nothing she could do. Only the black of night and the howl of the icy wind coursing through the street outside.

Her magic had failed her. Again.

So she paced and cursed, boot heels ringing against the floor as she curled her fingers into fists and ground her nails into her palms, doing the thing she hated most in the world. Waiting.

Rosa gasped, her entire body arching like a taught bow. Her eyes flicked open, wide open. So wide Val could see the whites all the way around.

"Rosa?"

She knelt beside her friend and reached out her hand, but pulled back at the last moment. Rosa's eyes were open, yet she wasn't seeing Val, or the half-crumbled garage, or the dark clouds above. Her mind was elsewhere.

She was having a vision. Whatever she was seeing, it was not here.

Rosa's lips began to move, making sounds so soft that Val wasn't even sure if they were words.

"What was that?"

Val turned her head and leaned closer, pushing her ear so close it almost brushed Rosa's lips. The soft whispering became words.

"The contract has not been honored. It was promised. The reckoning is at hand."

Rosa's voice faded away, becoming softer and softer until it trailed into inaudible breaths. Her lips continued to move, but no matter how hard Val strained her ears, she couldn't make out any more words. She sat back on her heels with a sigh.

"Well, that doesn't sound great."

When it became clear Rosa wasn't going to wake up yet, Val rose and resumed her pacing. She was tired and hungry, and starting to feel lightheaded and punchy. As she turned Rosa's words over in her head, her brain started to spin in random directions.

Why were prophecies always so foreboding? It was always doom and gloom and the world ending next Tuesday unless somebody did something to stop it. And 'somebody' usually meant Val.

Just once she wished a seer would predict that next Tuesday chocolate cupcakes would rain from the sky. Or the city would be overrun by playful kittens. Or the mayor decreed there would be free bubble bath for everyone going forward. Those were the types of prophecies she could get behind.

But no. It was always vampire covens or mad seraphim or a fae army coming to slaughter everyone in their path unless Val figured out how to close their magic portal. It was exhausting.

Rosa gave another gasp and sat up, breaking Val out of her increasingly random train of thought.

Rosa's gaze focused on Val, her eyes filled with the kind of wild certainty that was the special province of madmen and prophets. A triumphant grin split her features.

"I know where we need to go." Then she groaned and rubbed at her lower back. "Also, ow. Every muscle in my body feels like it's been beaten with a hammer. Why do visions have to hurt so much?"

---

They walked east for several blocks, the streets twisting and turning, growing narrower as they approached the hills. Full night had fallen, and it was now pitch dark. Low, gray clouds blocked any light the moon and stars might have provided, and there were no streetlights in this part of town. There wasn't even much ambient light from lighted windows, as most of the houses were either rubble or so badly damaged that they were uninhabited. In fact, there wasn't a single light or window shining. In the middle of a large city, this was eerie, to say the least.

Despite the darkness, Rosa marched confidently along, her eyes blazing with revelation. Val had to use Mister E's eyes to see through the gloom, but Rosa effortlessly matched her steps. Rosa's excitement was contagious, and Val found herself grinning along. She noticed that the two of them seemed oddly synchronized, like women living together who ended up on the same cycle, and she wondered if Rosa's new abilities went beyond her prophetic dreams.

Could she see in the dark now? Cast spells like Val? Who knew with fae magic?

The fae were renowned for being capricious, and their gifts were as unpredictable as they were. At least, Rosa was able to keep up with her in the dark — a relief, because it meant Val didn't have to babysit her. One less thing to worry about.

A gentle rain started to fall, little more than a mist, moistening her face, beading on her jacket and the tips of her hair. Val ignored it, the shared excitement coursing through her. A little water couldn't get her down now. Not when they were so close.

It felt like this case had been nothing but tedious legwork. Painstakingly tracing clues from one person to the next. Chaining events together in the hope that they would lead somewhere.

Sometimes things like that ended up going nowhere. You traipsed all over the city, interviewing people for days, only to find yourself at a dead end. Then you had to start all over again. Tug another thread. Figure out where that one took you instead.

But this time, the grunt work had paid off. Or Rosa's prophetic sight had. Val liked to think Rosa's vision had been prompted by the effort that had led to that moment, though. Talking to the Goblin Queen and Giselle and Miranda had metaphysically primed the pump.

Val could feel Rosa's hope beside her, burning in her friend's chest, so bright she could practically see it shining in the dark. She couldn't imagine what Rosa had been through over the past weeks. Nights of terror, tormented by ghastly visions. Exhausted days filled with anxiety. Not sleeping, not eating. Wasting away with every breath.

Val hoped that was all behind Rosa now. Her vision had finally given them a direction. They were zeroing in on Jorge's position. Soon the long nightmare would be over.

Rosa's steps faltered to a halt in front of a dark hole between two houses. They were part of a row that backed into the hillside, their basements and lower levels burrowing into the soil. Behind and above them, the rocky hill rose steeply, the surface covered with stubborn succulents, rocky outcroppings, and the gnarled sagebrush that had covered this land since long before people had ever set foot on the peninsula.

"Is this the right place?" Val asked uncertainly.

"This is where my vision leads," Rosa answered.

A chain-link fence divided the street from a freshly excavated foundation, gaping like a raw wound in the hillside. A metal sign on the fence read: *No Entry. Cathedral Construction Co.* Val couldn't decide whether a house there had been demolished and cleared away, or whether someone had now decided to fill a gap in the row of houses.

Either way, there was currently no sign of a structure. Just a black maw in the hillside, so dark that Val couldn't see more than a couple feet into it, even with Mister E's eyes. The darkness had a heavy presence, like something old. Val had the uncomfortable feeling that it was watching them.

"Are you sure this is it? It's just a vacant lot. I don't see Jorge," Val ventured.

"I don't either. But our path leads into the hillside. There must be more to that hole than we can see. Come on." Rosa ducked in through a gap in the fence.

Val followed, then put a hand on her shoulder. "Better let me take point. It's dark, and we don't know what's in there."

After a moment's hesitation, Rosa nodded and moved aside, one hand latching on to the sleeve of Val's jacket. Together, they stepped into the darkness.

# 31

"This is private property." A gruff voice rang out of the darkness. Val froze.

A man clutching an assault rifle stepped out from the hillside, where she now noticed a tiny guard shack. He must have been huddling inside, trying to stay dry. He didn't point the gun at them but kept the muzzle pointed at the dirt near his feet, for which Val was grateful. Having a gun pointed at you was never a good time. Particularly one that could chew you in half in seconds.

Val held her hands out in front of her, palms forward, moving slowly so as not to startle the man with any sudden movements.

"We don't want any trouble."

"You can't be here," the man said.

Val licked her lips, mind churning as she frantically tried to come up with a story on the spot.

"Sorry, we just wanted to get out of the rain. We saw the overhang and thought…" She trailed off, knowing how weak her story sounded.

*"Just bat your eyes at him and show some cleavage."* Mister E laughed. *"It would give you a better chance than the bullshit you're spewing."*

"It's a little cold out for that," Val shot back under her breath. "Also batting my eyes isn't really my strong suit."

"Move along." The guard gestured with the gun. "I don't care where you go, but you can't be here. This is private property."

"It must be pretty special to merit an armed guard," Rosa said. "Whose property is it?"

She stepped forward and batted her eyes, attempting to do the very thing that Mister E had just suggested. Unfortunately, the ambulatory skeleton look only worked for supermodels. Rosa just looked sickly. The guard took a step back and leveled his rifle at her emaciated chest. His voice became hard.

"Stop right there. Back away. This is your only warning. Don't make me shoot you."

Rosa's eyes grew wide and she took two quick steps back, raising her hands over her head

"I'm sorry. Please don't shoot me."

The fear in her voice was so genuine that the guard's face twisted with embarrassment. He lowered the muzzle of his gun.

That put him right where Val wanted him. While the man's attention was on Rosa, she had carefully sidled up to his flank. Now she struck.

Val lunged forward and hip-checked the man's rifle, knocking the barrel firmly aside while getting her body in the way of his targeting arc. She twisted and chopped down at his wrist, breaking his grip and making him drop the gun.

He swore and tried to grab her, but she gripped his arm and yanked the man off balance. As he stumbled forward, she spun around behind him and locked her arms around his neck in a chokehold. Thirty seconds later he went limp, and she dropped his unconscious body in front of the guard shack.

Rosa gaped at her. "Did you do that all without using magic?"

Val shrugged. "Magic is just a tool. It's far from the only one I have in my toolbox. Help me find something to tie this guy up with. We don't want him waking up and coming after us. Or, even worse, calling in reinforcements."

They rummaged around in the guard shack and found some rope.

"How are you with knots?" Val asked.

Rosa grinned. "Surprisingly good. When I was little, my cousin

Armando used to force me to play the damsel in distress. He would tie me up so he could pretend to come rescue me. I got tired of that shit real fast, so I got a book of knots from the library and turned the tables on him. I left him tied to a tree in the woods behind my *tía*'s house for six hours one day. He never tried to tie me up again."

"Great, because my knots are shit." Val tossed Rosa the rope. "It's about time that misspent youth came in handy."

Val held her hands out in front of her as she felt her way over the rocky, uneven ground. Rosa clutched the back of her jacket. Even with Mister E's eyes, the darkness in the shadow of the hillside was too heavy to see through. It felt thick with time, like molasses congealed at the bottom of a bottle.

Just take it slow, she told herself. One foot in front of the other.

After what seemed like an eternity, and long past the point where they should have walked right into the hillside, Val noticed that it had stopped raining. A few steps further in and the darkness began to lift ever so slightly, as if they were pushing through a blackout curtain and emerging behind the stage.

Then they stepped through and found themselves in an expansive cavern, stretching back into the hollow reaches of the hillside.

"What the fuck," Rosa whispered.

"You took the words right out of my mouth."

The massive cave had definitely not been made by men. The walls were uneven and jagged. Stalactites stretched down from the ceiling high overhead, groping toward matching stalagmite mounds on the cave floor. There was no telling how deep it went; the limits of the cave were lost in the darkness. Val could see recessed openings in the walls that suggested tunnels or other caves branching off to the sides. She also noticed something else.

"Take a look at this," she whispered. She didn't know why she was whispering. Something about the heavy silence of the cave seemed to demand it.

Elegant carvings scrolled around the mouth of a side tunnel to her left, outlining the opening with a delicate touch.

"Alien artifacts," Rosa whispered, echoing what Miranda had told them.

"I don't think so." Val stepped closer to get a better look. "I think these might be Native American carvings. They were probably left here by the people who lived on this peninsula before the Europeans arrived and killed them all off."

She ran a fingertip over the carvings, carefully tracing the strange geometric shapes.

"Do you think this could be some sort of writing?"

'I don't know," Rosa replied. "But my vision says we need to go through that doorway."

"Color me unsurprised," Val muttered as she stepped through the opening. She drew her knife. The weight of the steel was comforting in her grip. "Stay close. There could be anything in here."

Unlike the cave, the walls beyond the carvings were smooth and straight. Manmade.

"Why do I suddenly feel like Indiana Jones?" Rosa asked.

"I don't know, but if a giant ball of rock comes rolling down this tunnel, you'd better be ready to run like hell."

## 32

The tunnel burrowed deep into the bedrock. It smelled musty and old, and the ancient, oppressive silence was so heavy Val found herself holding her breath as they slowly moved forward.

"Watch out for tripwires," she whispered. "If there's one thing I've learned from the movies, it's that these places are full of tripwires."

"Don't forget about the booby-trapped flagstones," Rosa whispered back. "If a stone starts to sink under your foot, duck, because there are definitely poisoned darts coming out of the walls."

Val chuckled, but the banter was a false front. Gallows humor. In truth, she was terrified for no good reason that she could see. Something about this place made her instincts scream danger. And she trusted her instincts. They'd kept her alive so far.

The passage opened into a small chamber. More carvings covered the wall behind a small stone platform. Small and seemingly random objects had been placed on the platform: a quartz crystal, a rough wooden flute, a trio of obsidian arrowheads, some dust that might have once been flowers.

"An altar?" Val wondered.

"Seems like a good guess."

"Is this where your vision told you we need to come?" Val peered around the small stone chamber uncertainly. Aside from another arch of carvings behind the platform, there was nothing else to see.

Rosa bit her lip.

"No. There must be something beyond this. We have to figure out how to get there."

"How to get through solid stone? I'm sorry, but I think that's beyond my powers. Unless you've got a few thousand years. In that case, I'll call up some wind and start carving."

Rosa rolled her eyes.

"No, I mean there's another way. A secret door or something. You know, some Indiana Jones shit."

"Oh, right. Of course." Val's lips twisted as she scanned the blank walls around them. She muttered under her breath to Mister E. "Do you see anything?"

*"I see many things. Mostly, I see a pair of witches in over their heads. You do know who owns Cathedral Construction, yes?"*

"The sign on the fence?" Val asked distractedly, running her fingertips over the wall carvings. There had to be some way through. She just needed to find the trigger.

*"Yes, the sign on the fence. The company whose property you are now trespassing on."*

"Does it matter? We're trespassing, I get it. Rosa's vision said we needed to get in here, so we did. I don't see how it matters whose property we're trespassing on. We'll deal with the consequences later."

*"Mayor Light."* The cat drew the words out, tasting each syllable. *"That's who owns Cathedral Construction. That's who you're messing with here. The man who runs this entire city."*

That did give Val pause, but she tried to shrug it off.

"Why am I not surprised? Well, there's nothing we can do about it now. What's done is done and we'll deal with that when we have to. Or maybe we won't have to. We did tie up the guard, after all. If we're lucky, we'll be able to slip back out once we're done in here with no one the wiser."

Mister E laughed. *"Yes, because best case scenarios are so often the way things work around here."*

Val pushed his concern away and concentrated on the task at hand. One thing at a time.

She felt around the wall for hidden seams, feeling faintly ridiculous. Ancient ruins and secret chambers. Who came up with this stuff?

"Are they ruins if they're perfectly preserved?" she mused.

"What?" Rosa asked. She was kneeling beside the altar, poking around the base.

"If an ancient thing is perfectly preserved and not crumbling, is it still considered a ruin? I mean, this place is hardly ruined. It probably looks the same as it did a thousand years ago, or whenever it was the natives carved it out of the mountainside."

"Um, I don't know. I think they're probably still considered ruins. What else would you call it?"

"Cultural heritage sites?"

Rosa snorted.

"As long as you find the way through to the next chamber, you can call it whatever you want, Val. Can we focus, please? We're so close to finding my nephew it makes my back itch with impatience."

Val obligingly turned back to the carvings, kneeling as she worked her way down toward the floor. The wall was coated with a thin layer of dust. She sneezed, and a little cloud of it puffed into the air. The dirt of the ages, she thought, waving the cloud away from her face.

She was about to comment on it when she noticed something. The dust had been rubbed away over a pair of symbols near the bottom of the arch. She traced them with her fingertips, muttered a quick wish for luck, and pushed.

The pair of tile-sized blocks of stone clicked into the wall. She held her breath as some kind of counterweight *thunked* somewhere behind the stone. A moment later, the entire section of carved wall swung inward, revealing a secret chamber behind the altar.

"Indiana Jones shit," she breathed, looking at Rosa with wide eyes.

"That's the place." Rosa grinned, her face blazing with excitement. "That's where we need to go."

Val returned her smile and nodded.

"You ready?"

"I'm ready."

Together they stepped around the altar and into the secret chamber.

It was small; not much larger than a walk-in closet, really. And, like a closet, the chamber appeared to be a storage space.

Unlike a closet, this chamber was storing bones. Human bones.

Hundreds of human bones were set into the walls, held there with what Val guessed was a layer of clay. When the builders had run out of wall space for their macabre mosaic, they had started putting the bones on the floor. Piles of bones as high as her knee were stacked against all three walls. They looked ancient, dried and cracked with age.

But the piled bones weren't the thing that drew Val's eye. No. What caught her attention was the body lying in the middle of the room.

# 33

Rosa rushed to the body and knelt beside it. Tears streamed down her cheeks as she cradled the limp head in her hands.

"No no no no no." She seemed unaware of the words streaming past her lips. "This isn't right. You're supposed to be alive. My vision told me you were alive."

Val reached the obvious conclusion. Their quest was at its end. This was the body of Rosa's nephew, Jorge.

She stood staring down at her friend, feeling utterly useless. She had failed. Jorge was dead. Yet another person who had departed this world on her watch. Another dead body on her conscience.

She wanted to comfort Rosa, console her in some way. But she had no idea how to even begin.

One would think that with all her experience with death she would be better at this. That she would know what to do in such situation. What to say. She should have some stock phrases ready to go. Blandly comforting sentiments that would make no one feel better, but that were nevertheless expected at times like these. Words that proved you were putting in an effort. Being a good friend.

But nothing came to her. Should she put her arms around Rosa? Pat

her on the back? Whisper 'there, there' as if either of them had any idea
what the fuck those words even meant?

She became aware of the hot rage building in her chest. Her hands
balled into fists. She wanted to hit something. Someone. Find whoever
was responsible for this and make them pay. That was the only way
Val knew to offer comfort.

Through action, not words.

But here, now, at this moment, as Rosa cradled Jorge's body in her
arms and wailed, tears dripping from her chin, all Val's possible
actions felt pointless. Futile. Every bit as empty as those meaningless,
comforting words.

So she stood there, clenching and unclenching her fists as time
passed, paralyzed by her inability to do or say a single useful thing.

Unable to help her friend, she found herself examining the room
instead. Working the case. It was fairly small, maybe eight feet square.
The bones stacked up around the edges made it feel even smaller.
There were hundreds of them. Hundreds of complete skeletons. People
entombed here for eternity.

The bones inlaid into the walls were particularly fascinating. It
looked like the people who made the room had spread a layer of soft
clay over the stone and pressed the bones into it, creating patterns
every bit as intricate and inscrutable as the ones on the stone arches
around the doorways. Every type of bone had been used, from the
stark, long strokes of femurs to tiny, intricate whirls created using delicate hand and foot bones. Some of them had even been fashioned into
clouds and raindrops falling down the wall. As her eyes traced the
patterns, she realized they all seemed to sweep towards the floor.

Following the motion of the designs, Val finally noticed the floor.
Shamed by her inability to offer comfort to her friend, she'd been
avoiding looking down. Distracting herself by letting her eyes roam
everywhere except there.

But now she finally realized that a thick layer of bones had been
inlaid into the floor as well, creating a macabre kind of tile. She cocked
her head, following the lines and whorls. It was actually a mosaic, the
place where all the wall designs came together, swirling into a grand
pattern. A circle. A magic circle.

And Jorge's body was lying in the center of it.

Her investigative brain kicked into overdrive as she started to notice more details. Jorge's hands and feet were splayed out like the points of a star. His throat had been slit.

This wasn't just a murder. It was a ritual. Jorge had been sacrificed.

"Do you recognize any of these patterns?" she whispered under her breath. "Can you tell me what they mean? Who made them?"

Mister E appeared, floating near the wall. He was wearing a top hat, his candy cigarette in a long ivory holder, a golden monocle over his left eye. He squinted at the patterns and puffed thoughtfully on his cigarette, making thinking noises and looking every bit like a classic detective on a case. Val suppressed the urge to roll her eyes.

Finally, he harrumphed officiously. *"I believe this to be the work of the Ohlone tribe, the native people who inhabited this peninsula for thousands of years before the arrival of the Spaniards."*

"Do you have any idea what it means? Why Jorge was sacrificed here?"

The cat puffed and squinted some more before declaring, *"I have no idea whatsoever."*

Val sighed. "Well at least we know who built the room. I guess that's something to go on. More than we knew before, at any rate."

Eventually Rosa's wails became whimpers. The whimpers faded to whispers, then to silence.

Val cautiously said, "I'm so sorry, Rosa."

"I just don't understand," her friend said in an exhausted, dazed voice. "My vision told me he was alive. Why would it lie to me?"

"I don't know. Maybe he was still alive when you had the vision?"

"Maybe."

But Val could tell that neither of them really believed it. The bloody line across Jorge's throat was dry and crusted. He had been dead for days.

"We'll find them," Val promised. "We'll find whoever did this and make them pay."

## 34

They debated whether it would be better to carry Jorge's body out with them, or if they should leave it where they'd found it and call the police. In the end, they decided summoning the police was the wiser course. It was a murder scene, after all.

As they stumbled out of the cave, they were surprised to find the police already waiting for them. Or at least a version of the police. Cathedral Construction security, to be precise. They stepped out into the glare of floodlights and a hard voice barked commands over a bullhorn.

"Come out with your hands up. Don't make any sudden movements."

Squinting into the light, Val saw at least three guards with guns silhouetted against the bulk of a security van. She thought one of them was the man they had left tied up, but it was hard to be sure with the floodlights behind him.

"So much for your knots," she muttered.

"Sorry, it was a long time ago," Rosa said in a soft monotone. She looked shell-shocked and dazed, her expression lost.

"Up against the fence," the man with the bullhorn ordered. "Keep your hands where I can see them. Hands on the fence."

"We found a dead body in there. It's her nephew. You need to call the police," Val called out.

"Hands on the fence," the man repeated.

Val frowned. She didn't want to antagonize the man, but she also didn't have a lot of patience for rent-a-cops.

"Can you just call the real police?" she asked, in what she thought was a remarkably civil tone.

The three men with the guns clearly didn't like her implying that they weren't real police, because they leveled their guns at her.

"This is your last warning. Hands on the fence. Now."

Val heard a safety click off.

"Fine. No need to get so worked up about it."

She and Rosa did as they were told. One of the security guards stepped forward and frisked them while the other two kept their distance, guns trained on their backs.

*"It looks like they've learned not to get too close to you,"* Mister E observed. *"I guess old dogs can learn new tricks."*

"That's not the only trick I have," Val muttered.

"Quiet!" the nearest guard snapped. He hauled Val's left arm down behind her back and snapped a handcuff around her wrist.

"Seriously?" Val protested, struggling as he grabbed her other arm. "I'm not going to just let you…"

Pain exploded in the side of her head as one of the other guards stepped forward and cracked the butt of his rifle against her skull. The world went dark.

By the time she got her senses back, she was on a bench in the back of the van, with both wrists cuffed behind her back. Rosa sat next to her in the same state, staring dully forward. One of the guards sat across from them, his eyes hard.

*"That guard must still be upset with you for choking him out on the way in."* Mister E chuckled.

"Ow," Val moaned. Pain shot through her skull, smearing her vision with blobs of color. "I think I might have a concussion."

The van lurched into motion beneath them, causing her to nearly fall on Rosa.

"Where are you taking us?" she demanded. 'Demanded' was probably too strong a word. Speaking hammered spikes of pain through her skull, and her voice came out as more of a croak.

The guard ignored her, keeping his eyes fixed on the wall above her head, so she tried again.

"Hey. Where are you taking us? You can't just force people into your van. This is kidnapping."

The guard glared at her, and for a moment she thought he was going to hit her again. She belatedly realized he was the guard she'd choked out earlier. Yeah, she probably wasn't going to find much sympathy there.

To her surprise, he decided to answer her question.

"We're taking you in for trespassing on city property."

"City property?" Val croaked. "But that site was…"

"Shut up!" the guard barked, raising the butt of his rifle threateningly. "I'm not going to sit here and listen to your mouth the whole way. You shut it, or I'll shut it for you. Your choice."

Val did as she was told. Her head hurt enough as it was. If he hit her again, she was afraid her skull would split like an egg and dribble brains all over the van.

She wondered at his words. How could that lot be city property? It was a lot under development on a residential street, surrounded by houses. As far as she knew, the city didn't build houses like that. Not that she was an expert on the subject by any means. Maybe they did, and she simply didn't know about it.

Still, it felt strange.

"Are you all right?" she whispered to Rosa, keeping one eye on the guard.

"No, I'm not all right," her friend answered. "My nephew is dead and these stupid visions have been keeping me awake and lying to me for weeks. None of it is all right."

"I'm sorry. We'll find the people who killed him."

"That won't help. He'll still be dead."

Val didn't know what to say to that. It was true, but she couldn't bring Jorge back from the dead. Justice was the only thing she had to offer.

The van drove for maybe fifteen minutes before the sound of the tires on the asphalt changed. It became smooth and squeaky around the corners, while the noises around them became hollow echoes.

Val perked up. They were inside something, or perhaps underground. Maybe a parking garage.

Her suspicions were proven right when the van rolled to a stop and the back doors swung open. The guard prodded them out, and they had to do an awkward hop down without the use of their hands to steady themselves. Sure enough, they were in a big underground parking garage.

The guard took them to a small room with blank walls containing only a spare table and some chairs. He seated them on one side of the table, removed their cuffs and left them alone. The lock clicked home as the guard closed the door behind him on his way out.

"Well, this is an interrogation room if I've ever seen one," Val observed with a sigh. "One guess what happens next."

Rosa said nothing. She stared straight ahead and ignored all Val's attempts at further conversation.

They sat and waited for so long that Val's ass went to sleep and her bladder started to complain.

Finally, a nondescript man in a gray suit came into the room. Closing the door, he stood and stared at them for a long minute without saying a word. He looked like a million faceless bureaucrats the world over. She felt there was something familiar about the man, though she couldn't put her finger on what, exactly. Val wanted to snap at him, but she sensed that was what he wanted, so she just glowered.

At last, his thin lips curved into a hint of a smile that didn't reach his ice-blue eyes.

"This can go easy or this can be difficult and painful," he said in a voice as mild as pond water. "Now, why don't you tell me what you were doing at our construction site?"

# 35

Val considered lying to the man, but what would be the point? Jorge's body was still inside the cave, and if the company's guards hadn't found him already, they would soon. Given that she and Rosa actually wanted Jorge's body found, and had nothing to hide, the truth seemed like a no-brainer.

"We were looking for my friend's nephew. He's been missing for several days," she said.

The man made no reaction, his expression remaining vanilla-bland.

"Why were you trespassing on our property?" he asked.

"I just told you. We were looking for her nephew."

"That doesn't answer my question."

"I think it does."

"No," he said slowly, as if explaining something to a three-year-old. "It doesn't. It explains why you were in the area, perhaps. But it doesn't explain why you assaulted one of our guards and broke into our building site."

"Well, we did ask nicely, but he wouldn't let us in. In fact, he pointed his gun at us, which I personally thought was pretty rude."

"So you took that as an opportunity to…"

"To invite ourselves in. As I'm sure you can tell, my friend has been sick with worry. She hasn't been eating or sleeping. I wasn't going to let some frat boy working as part-time security stop us from finding her nephew."

The man regarded Val silently for a several long seconds. Finally, he sighed.

"You don't have much respect for authority, do you Miss Keri?"

"Authority hasn't..." she began, but then realized what the man had said. "How do you know my name?"

"I know many things, Miss Keri. But I'm the one asking the questions here." He paused and folded his hands together. He opened his mouth to say something, closed it as he reconsidered his words. Finally, he said, "Why do you believe you are above the law, Miss Keri?"

"I don't. I just..."

"Clearly, you do, Miss Keri. If you did not, you would be more hesitant about assaulting a security guard and breaking into private property. I would go so far as to say that most people wouldn't even consider these actions, yet they are actions you not only considered but acted on without hesitation. Even now, when confronted with your actions, you are neither ashamed nor apologetic. Why is that, if you do not consider yourself above the law?"

Val stared at the man.

"I think you're missing the point. Rosa's nephew is dead. Murdered. We found his body inside your 'property.' I would think you'd be a lot more concerned about that than my lack of respect for authority."

"So you admit that you lack respect for authority."

"Look, you little shit—" Val exploded.

She hated people like him. Bland bureaucrats who loved to twist words and win arguments with loopholes and technicalities. In her experience, such people rarely cared about what was objectively good or evil; all they cared about was the law. Or, more specifically, all the ways they could twist the law to suit their own ends.

The man in the suit didn't flinch.

"You prove my point with every passing second," he said.

"A man is dead!"

"People die every day." He said this in the same way he might have said: The sky is blue. "That is not my concern."

"Not your concern? For someone so concerned about his 'private property,' you sure don't seem to give a shit about what happens on it. Unless someone happens to be trespassing, of course; then you give a lot of shits."

"What is your interest in Mayor Light?" he asked abruptly.

"I... what?" Val stammered, taken aback by the change of topic.

"You were seen at two of the mayor's rallies. Both of which turned violent. Given your predilection toward violence, I can't say that I'm surprised you would be present at such things." He leaned forward, placing his hands flat on the table. "Why were you there?"

"I don't see what this has to do with Jorge lying dead inside that cave," Val snapped. "What I do with my free time is none of your business."

"Isn't it?" He raised a thin eyebrow at her. "I will leave you to ponder the answer to that question for a while. We shall resume this conversation when I return."

Before Val could protest, the man swept out of the room. As the door swung shut behind him, she heard him say to someone she couldn't see, "Get me the mayor."

# 36

"The mayor? What was all that about?" Val wondered. When neither Rosa nor Mister E replied, she looked up at the ceiling and sighed. "No one? Just me talking to myself? Wonderful."

*"You have a knack for catching the attention of powerful people."* Mister E appeared, floating on his back in mid-air, striped tail flicking and curling. *"Maybe you should go into politics."*

"Funny. I would make the world's worst politician. Being tactful isn't one of my strengths."

*"Whoever said politicians need to be tactful? There is a certain type of politician who gathers support by being just the opposite. People gravitate to them because they say things out loud that others only dare to think. Mayor Light is a perfect example of this. He gives voice to people's secret fears and hatreds. Because of this, people feel that he understands them."*

"So you're saying people like him because he understands that they are secretly paranoid and hateful?"

*"Yes. And by understanding them, he gives them permission to be those things. Instead of condemning them for their faults, he embraces them and gives them a voice. At heart, everyone wants to be loved and accepted, just the way they are."*

"I'd say the same thing about the shifters they target with their lynch mobs."

*"And you would be right. But I don't think the mayor's supporters see it that way. Self-awareness isn't one of their strengths."*

"Or maybe it is and they just don't care."

*"Also a possibility."*

In the chair beside Val, Rosa went rigid. Every muscle in her body snapped taut and she started to convulse, eyes rolling up into the back of her head until only the whites were showing. Blood trickled out between Rosa's lips, dripping off the end of her chin.

"Shit, she's having a seizure. I think she bit her tongue. Guard!" Val called. "We need some help in here!"

She hesitated, trying to think. What should you do in these situations? She thought that maybe you were supposed to shove something in the victim's mouth to keep them from choking or biting their tongue. Judging by the blood, it looked like it was too late for that. Also, she didn't have a belt or something else handy to shove between Rosa's grinding teeth. In desperation, she tried to pry open Rosa's mouth and wedge the sleeve of her leather jacket between her lips.

*"Stop that. You aren't supposed to do that,"* Mister E said. *"You could hurt her."*

"Well, what am I supposed to do?"

*"Just keep her safe and wait. Call for help."*

"I did that already. Guard!" she called again.

*"Stay calm. Most seizures only last a few minutes. Sit with her and make sure she doesn't hurt herself."*

"You're an expert on prophetic seizures now?"

*"I know lots of things,"* the cat smirked.

Rosa made a horrible choking sound and Val tensed, her hands opening and closing helplessly, wanting to help her friend, but not knowing how. Then Rosa's friend's eyes bulged and she stopped breathing.

"Guard! Help!"

Rosa's mouth wasn't opening. And now it looked like she had swallowed her tongue.

She glanced at the door in panic. Still no guards. She was on her own.

Rosa's lips were starting to turn blue.

"What do I do? I can't sit here and do nothing!" Tears of frustration streamed down Val's cheeks. "I don't want to hurt her, but I won't watch her die either."

*"Lay her down and turn her on her side. Put something soft under her head."*

She grabbed Rosa under the arms and prepared to lift … just as Rosa stopped struggling. Her friend went completely limp, her head flopping back, mouth falling open. Rosa's chest spasmed as she sucked in a big breath.

"Oh, thank the gods." Val slumped back, exhausted. She felt like she'd run ten miles in the last two minutes.

Rosa moaned and began to stir.

"Take it easy," Val said. "You just had a seizure."

"I know." Rosa's voice was thick. "I bit my tongue."

Val winced.

"Sorry about that. I tried to stop you, but your jaw was locked so tight I would have had to break it to get it open. When you stopped breathing, I thought I was going to have to do just that. Fortunately, you stopped convulsing before I had to."

"Thank you," Rosa said softly.

She opened her eyes and Val recoiled. The whites of Rosa's eyes were red with blood, as if every capillary had burst simultaneously.

Rosa didn't notice Val's reaction. She worried her lip with her teeth and stared straight ahead, as if she were focused on something a thousand miles away.

"I had another vision, but I don't understand it."

"What was it?"

"I saw Jorge. Alive. Cloaked in shadows and pain."

"But he's dead. We saw his body."

Rosa leaned forward and groaned, burying her face in her hands.

"I know. It makes no sense."

"Could it have been just a dream?" Val ventured. "Wishful thinking?"

"If I was sleeping, I'd say yes. But I wasn't sleeping. This was a powerful vision, one of the strongest I've ever had. I can't explain it, but I *know* it was true."

Val's forehead creased.

"Well, I know of at least one way someone can be dead but not dead," she began, thinking of Malcolm and Hillary. "But it can't be that, because we saw Jorge's body. I don't know of any way someone can be undead without a body. Unless… he was a ghost?"

"No." Rosa shook her head. "He wasn't a ghost. He was still alive."

"Still alive without his body? That's a new one." Val muttered under her breath, "Any insights, furball?"

*"It's certainly possible,"* Mister E peered up at the ceiling through his monocle. *"After all, I am Exhibit A."*

"That's true. You don't have a body, do you?"

*"Well, I do. I just have to share it with an angry witch."* He smirked.

"Funny. Do you think that's what's happened? Is Jorge somehow sharing someone else's body?"

*"How should I know? Anything is possible."*

Val noticed Rosa staring at her. Her cheeks flushed as she realized how she must look, talking to the invisible cat.

"Sorry. Just thinking out loud. I talk to myself when I'm trying to figure things out."

Rosa waved her explanation away.

"Talking to yourself is the least strange thing I've seen today. Did you come to any conclusions?"

"The best theory I can come up is that maybe Jorge's spirit is still alive, but somehow he's sharing someone else's body. Would that make sense with your vision?"

Rosa frowned, her eyes going distant again as she thought.

"Maybe…" she said slowly. "I'm not sure. Something about it doesn't feel quite right."

The door swung open, cutting their discussion short. Mayor Light stepped into the room.

# 37

Mayor Light glided into the room on a million-dollar smile. Up close, his eyes were the impossible blue of glacial ice. Looking into them, Val felt as if she were falling. But not for long. The mayor's smile caught her in a warm embrace, setting her gently back on her feet. His expression said, "I see you. And I understand." A wave of dizziness swept over her and she had to extend her hands out to the sides to keep from toppling over.

All this without saying a word.

The man in the gray suit followed the mayor, and Val suddenly realized why he'd looked so familiar. He'd been onstage holding a clipboard, standing behind the mayor at the rally outside the Mission Shifter Settlement.

Then Mayor Light spoke, and all thoughts of the gray man were swept out of her head.

"Charles Light. It's a pleasure to meet you." His smile grew brighter as he extended a hand.

Val took it without question. His skin was soft and warm, and when their fingers touched an electric charge ran up her arm, tingling all the way across her scalp. His blue eyes never left hers. Her cheeks grew warm.

"Val Keri."

"I know. My people have told me quite a bit about you, Miss Keri."

"About me?" she stammered. "But I'm nobody."

"Don't be so modest, Val. May I call you Val?" She felt her head nod automatically. "Well, Val, you are a celebrity on your own right. My people tell me you've been making quite a name for yourself."

"I have?"

"You've been making waves. Running with some of our finest citizens. Padraig O'Ceallaigh. Joumala Anand. The late Zoe Vasilevski."

*"'Finest citizens' must be code for 'richest citizens,'"* Mister E snarked. Val ignored him. The demon cat's voice was faint and far away, like a fly buzzing at a window across the room.

"I wouldn't say I was running with them, exactly," she demurred. "Zoe Vasilevski was a client. I was investigating the murder of her uncle. I only interacted with the others as part of the investigation."

"Investigation is such an interesting word," the man in gray stepped forward, his eyes sharp. "Is it true that you are a private investigator? How does one get into that line of work?"

Val felt her flush deepen.

"I … I sort of fell into it," she stammered.

"And how does one 'fall into' private investigating?"

"Well, it wasn't really a conscious choice. A friend of mine was murdered and I felt like I needed to track down her killer. After that, people just started coming to me with their problems. One thing led to another and…" She gestured helplessly. "The next thing I know, I'm a private investigator."

"Have you had proper training for this job? Do you have a license?" The man in gray grilled her.

"Well, no, but…"

"So you're not so much a private investigator as a vigilante?"

"That's not fair, I…"

"Private investigators have to be licensed by the city, Miss Keri," the man's voice was hard. "You can't simply print up business cards and call yourself an investigator."

"OK, but…"

And," he continued, riding right over her, "you cannot trespass on someone's private property and claim to be investigating a missing person. There are laws against that sort of thing. Laws you would be aware of if you had a private investigator's license. Which you do not."

The mayor put his hand on the man's shoulder.

"I think that's enough, Roland," he said. "I believe Miss Keri understands the gravity of the situation."

The man in gray folded his arms across his chest.

"Does she? I'm not convinced. I think we should prosecute for trespassing."

Val's heart hammered. Sweat prickled across the back of her neck. She was already on SFPD's shit list. If the mayor's office decided to prosecute, things would not go well for her. Or Rosa, for that matter.

She cut her eyes to her friend and was surprised to find that Rosa didn't appear concerned or worried or frightened. In fact, the seer seemed completely unaware of the man in gray. Her dark eyes were intent upon Mayor Light, and they practically glowed with intensity. If looks could burn a hole through someone, the mayor would be smoking right now. Val wasn't sure what that look meant, but she thought she should try to defuse the situation before Rosa made things worse with one of her cryptic pronouncements.

"That won't be necessary," she said. "Simply return Jorge's body from the cave and you won't see us anymore."

"I'm afraid it's not that simple, Val." The mayor's expression was regretful as he turned his palms up in a what-are-you-going-to-do gesture.

"There will have to be an official investigation," the gray-suited man added. "These things take time."

"Time is one thing we do not have," Rosa pronounced.

Val winced. Rosa's voice had that spectral, haunted tone she used when she was relaying a vision.

"I don't believe we've been introduced," the mayor turned his attention to Rosa for the first time. Val felt him turn up the charm like a physical thing, as if he'd twisted the dial on some internal heat lamp.

Rosa seemed completely unaffected by the mayor's charisma, her dark sunken eyes not even glancing at him. Instead she stared straight ahead, looking every bit like an oracle stepping out of her mountaintop cave.

"The circle is broken. What was taken must be returned by the dawn of the full moon. Restore the balance, or the streets will run with blood."

Val frowned. The full moon was only two days away. Not much time to "restore the balance." Whatever that meant.

Mayor Light and the gray man exchanged looks. For the blink of an eye, the mayor looked uncertain. Did she detect a flicker of guilt in the mayor's expression? If so, it was there and gone so fast she half believed she'd imagined it. What in Rosa's prophecy could have provoked that?

"That's certainly an interesting statement." The mayor's smile slipped a bit. "Care to elaborate?"

Rosa finally looked right at him, her eyes burning with accusation.

"You know that of which I speak. Restore the balance. Return that which was taken."

Mayor Light flinched when their eyes met, and Val couldn't blame him. Rosa's bruised and sunken eyes showed blood-red whites all the way around, and her pupils were so large they'd swallowed her irises whole. With her gaunt features, she looked every inch the mad prophet. Which Val supposed she kind of was.

To her surprise, the mayor actually took a step back. He looked away, unable or unwilling to hold Rosa's stare. He cleared his throat and turned his eyes back to Val, gaze latching on to her like he was grabbing a lifeline.

"Yes, well. You certainly do keep fascinating company, Val." He dialed his smile back up, but it seemed brittle now. "I've got another appointment, so I'm afraid I'll have to leave Roland to help you get sorted out. It was wonderful meeting you."

He turned and swept out of the room without another word.

In sharp contrast to the mayor, the smile Roland gave them was thin and predatory.

"Yes," he said softly. "Let's get you all sorted out."

## 38

"Here's what's going to happen," Roland said. "We're going to let you go. You're going to walk out that door and we are never going to see you again."

Val and Rosa looked at one another.

"That's it?" Val asked.

"The mayor wants me to give you a chance. So I'm giving you a chance." Roland's mild tone was at odds with the cold gleam in his eyes. "Walk away. The mayor's business is above your pay grade, Miss Keri. Walk away and forget everything you discovered today. Go back to your little neighborhood. Back to your amateur 'investigations.' I'm going to open that door, you are going to walk out of it, and we will never see each other again."

"What about Jorge's body?"

"The body will be returned to the family in due course."

"In due course? And when is that?"

"After a proper investigation, naturally."

Val crossed her arms over her chest.

"An investigation by whom? By you?"

Roland's tone became withering, "By the SFPD. By the professionals. Amateur hour is over, Miss Keri. Go home." He turned to leave.

His dismissive attitude rubbed Val the wrong way. She called out, stopping him with his hand on the door.

"What if I don't?"

Roland looked back over his shoulder. His face could have been carved from granite.

"I wouldn't recommend that, Miss Keri. As I said, you are in over your head here. These are deep waters. People drown in them."

With that, the man was gone.

Rosa shuddered. "He is creepy."

"And he likes making threats entirely too much," Val agreed. "This whole thing stinks."

"Well, at least they're letting us go. That's not a bad thing, right?"

Val scowled. "They're brushing us aside. That means they're hiding something. I just wish I knew what it was."

A woman in a pink power suit opened the door, sweeping in on a cloud of blooming roses and morning dew. She was stunning, with the kind of curves 1950s pinup girls dreamed of and a face that would launch a thousand ships. Her smile was even brighter than the mayor's, which Val would have thought impossible.

"I'm so sorry for the inconvenience," she gushed. "If you'll follow me, we'll get you out of here."

When she spoke, Val's world went all soft-focus. She found herself grinning like a fool while nodding dumbly. She would follow this woman anywhere.

The next few minutes were a blur. The woman led them down tiled hallways under sterile strip lights and eventually into an office, where they signed some papers. Val didn't know what the papers were. She didn't bother to read them.

All her attention was on the woman in pink. She was the most beautiful creature Val had ever seen. She made the fae look drab and boring by comparison. All Val wanted was to be near her. To see her smile. To breathe the air that she breathed.

Sometime later Val found herself standing on the sidewalk, blinking as gray reality came crashing down around her. The sky was overcast in the dim half-light of early morning. A chill breeze swept down the street, carrying the scent of the sea and a faint mist that moistened her face and raised goosebumps across the back of her neck. Her time with the pink woman was only a warm blur in her mind, and an impossible sadness swept over her. The world was cold and gray and wet, and the woman was gone. Nothing would ever be good, ever again.

She looked to the side and was surprised to find Rosa standing there. She had forgotten all about her in the pink woman's vortex. Tears ran down Rosa's cheeks.

"She was so beautiful," Rosa whispered. "Like an angel."

"More like a devil, I think," Val said. "No one is that beautiful. She put us under some kind of spell. A charm."

She shook her head, trying to clear the cobwebs. Her brain told her what the woman must have done to them and her logical side was trying to be outraged, but her heart wasn't having it. Whenever she thought of the woman, warm adoration flowed through her. Whatever the woman had done to them, it was frighteningly powerful.

As the woman's power slowly drained away, exhaustion flowed in to take its place. Val swayed on her feet.

"What do we do now?" Rosa asked.

"We do what they said. Go home and get some rest."

"That's it? You're giving up the case?"

"You asked me to find Jorge. I did. The case is closed."

"But we found his body. How did he die? Who killed him? And what about my vision that said he's still alive? We can't just give up. We need answers."

"You need answers," Val corrected. "I need sleep. It's been a long day and a longer night. I don't even know how many hours I've been awake at this point. Too many."

She turned toward the corner. She wasn't sure exactly where they were. The large brick building they'd emerged from spanned the length of the entire block. They'd come out what appeared to be a side-entrance, and the featureless metal doors told her nothing. She would check the street signs at the intersection to get her bearings.

Rosa grabbed the sleeve of her leather jacket, tugging her to a halt.

"You can't just walk away. What about my vision? There's something bigger happening here. Jorge's death is only a part of it."

Val sighed and scrubbed her face with her hands.

"Look, I want to help. I do. But if you want to talk about your visions, you need come by the apartment later. And by later, I mean at least twelve hours from now. My everything hurts and my brain feels like it's been soaked in formaldehyde. I need to sleep for eleven of those hours before I can even start to process whatever it is you want me to do. I suggest you do the same."

"What time is it now?" Rosa called after her.

"Do I look like Big Ben? It's time to get a watch."

Val's stomach complained loudly as she weaved her way down the street, overwhelmed by her body's competing demands for sleep and food. She couldn't figure out which one she needed first. Was it possible to eat while sleeping? That sounded like the perfect solution.

## 39

When Val awoke, no chocolate pancakes were cooking. No rich scent of coffee brewing. No Malcolm singing Diana Ross in the kitchen.

The apartment was silent and entirely empty.

*That's weird. I wonder where everyone is.*

She blearily scooped coffee into the filter and stood swaying in the kitchen, groggily listening to the coffee maker burble to itself. Her stomach growled. She pulled open the refrigerator while she waited for the caffeine and squinted unhappily at the contents. The shelves were full, but none of the food was hers.

*Looks like I need to add shopping to my to-do list.*

Val contented herself with grabbing the butterscotch creamer and applying a liberal dose of it to her coffee. Cupping the steaming mug between her palms, she wandered out to the living room, enjoying the warmth of the coffee against the San Francisco evening chill.

She almost dropped her mug in surprise.

The living room walls were finished. Not just finished, but spackled and painted daffodil-yellow. The ceiling had been recoated in white. Even the baseboards had been replaced. The windows remained boarded up — she guessed they must still be waiting for the glass to come in — but other than that, there was no hint that the living room had ever been firebombed.

As she stood there gaping, the front door was flung open and Malcolm and Sandra swept into the room. Well, Malcolm swept; Sandra was pulled along in his wake like a paper boat tied to a string.

"We have arrived," Malcolm announced grandly. He looked like an incognito movie star, with oversized sunglasses and a silk scarf, a wide-brimmed Audrey Hepburn hat and black leather gloves. A pair of white paper shopping bags dangled from his arm. "No need to get up."

Val blinked at him from where she stood in the center of the living room.

"I'm already up."

Malcom rolled his eyes. "It's a figure of speech, Val. It means don't trouble yourself. Relax. Go about your business. Sprekenzie English?"

"Um. Yes." Val took a large slurp of her coffee. It would have been better if she'd had time to get a cup or two into her system before having to grapple with the whirlwind that was Malcolm.

He lowered his sunglasses and raised an eyebrow as he noticed her coffee and sleep-mussed hair.

"Did you just get up, Val? The sun is setting. I thought I was the vampire around here."

"Cut me some slack, Malcolm. I had a late night. I guess it was an early morning, really."

Malcolm smirked. "Oooo, do tell. Did you get your back scratched? Is there someone in your bedroom we should know about?"

Val rolled her eyes. "Not that kind of late night."

"Awww, and here I thought you might have finally broken your streak." He made a sad face but brightened up almost immediately and started digging into one of his bags. "I've got just the thing to brighten your celibate conjurer's soul. I brought goodies from Brown-ie's Bakery."

He pulled out a cardboard box, flipping the lid open with a flourish worthy of a stage magician. "Chocolate croissants, chocolate muffins, and some eclairs. Just what the doctor ordered to soothe your poor, lonely heart."

"My heart is not lonely," Val protested. She plucked a chocolate croissant from the box, nevertheless.

Malcolm patted her on the hand. "Shhhh, just eat the chocolate. Everything is going to be OK."

"How was the library?" Val asked, pointedly changing the subject.

"The library was fabulous, wasn't it, Sandra?" Malcolm asked, turning his smirk on a new target.

It was the gorgon's turn to look uncomfortable.

"Um, yeah. Great," she stammered, her cheeks flaming red around the edges of her mirrored sunglasses.

"The Librarian was very pleased to see our hot little monster," Malcolm said. "Who knew that fox onesie would bring all the girls to the yard?"

Sandra's face became so hot, Val thought she might spontaneously combust. She stepped in to rescue the poor girl.

"I meant the research, Malcolm. Not Sandra's love life. You did remember to do the research?"

"Spoilsport." He stuck his tongue out at her. "Yes, I did your research, Val. Of course I did. I just find Sandra's extra-curricular activities more interesting."

"And?" she prompted.

"Fine. If you insist on being all serious and boring." He sighed and flopped down on the couch before pulling a notebook from one of his bags. He made a show of flipping it open. "Let's see, what did we learn... Ah, yes. Ahem. The Rain King.

"First of all, I was unable to find any specific references to a Rain King, per se. I did, however, find lots of stuff about rain gods in this area. Historically speaking, California was not nearly as wet as it is today. In fact, most of the state has been pretty much a desert for centuries. Modern humans did their best to fight that with irrigation, but that didn't change the underlying conditions. So, as you can imagine, the people who lived here spent a lot of time praying to the rain god. Or gods, depending on their specific belief system. But usually it was a single god who was in charge of the rain."

He flipped a page before continuing.

"According to my research, this peninsula was occupied by the

Ohlone and Coast Miwok peoples before the Americans came and ruined everything. Well, technically the Spanish came and ruined everything first. Anyway, the Ohlone, who the Spanish called the Costanoans, had their own pantheon of gods and such, and one of their strongest gods was the one who ruled the weather. Or, in other words, the Rain King."

Malcolm paused dramatically.

When Val didn't react, he prompted, "This is the part where you thank me and tell me how great I am."

"You're great," she said absently.

Her mind was racing, thinking back to the chamber where they had found Jorge's body. The walls had been covered by Ohlone carvings. Jorge had been lying in a magic circle made of bone fragments. His throat had been slit.

Now Malcolm was saying he thought the Rain King was a native god.

"I think Jorge might have been sacrificed to the Rain King," she whispered.

Malcolm cocked his head at her.

"Well, that's a leap. I think I'm missing something here. Care to fill me in?"

Val quickly told him about the chamber and Jorge's ritual sacrifice.

"Ah, that makes more sense now," he acknowledged, shuddering. "You're right, it does sound like the poor guy was sacrificed. What a terrible way to go."

"The thing I still can't figure out is: Why? Why would someone want the Rain King to return? It's not like we lack rain. It rains here almost every day."

"Perhaps that's the reason," Sandra said softly. "Wouldn't a rain god be more powerful when it rains? So the Rain King would be one of the strongest gods you could summon these days."

Val pursed her lips. "That makes sense. Someone wanted to summon a powerful god, so they summoned the Rain King. That still leaves us with the question of why? Why summon a god at all? What did they want the god's power for?"

Malcolm and Sandra had no answers to that question. They all stared at each other blankly.

Right on cue, Rosa stepped in through the open front door, her prophetic eyes blazing.

"Who owned the property where the Rain King was summoned?" she asked. "Who warned us to stay out of their business?"

"The mayor." Val grimaced. "You're right. It all points back to Mayor Light."

## 40

"We need to go back to that construction site," Val said. "Hopefully they haven't moved Jorge's body yet. If we're going to find answers, that's the place to start."

Malcolm peered at Rosa.

"You know," he said, "you're really getting this whole mad prophet thing down. The sunken cheekbones. Burning eyes. Hair that looks like it hasn't been brushed in weeks. Sweeping in through the door and making dramatic pronouncements. Way to own it, girl."

Rosa remained focused on Val. It was unclear whether she'd even heard Malcolm.

"It's a long walk. We should get started." Rosa turned to the door.

"I might be able to help with that," Gunter said as he walked in carrying a large pane of glass.

Val threw up her hands. "Does anyone knock anymore?"

Gunter ducked his head. "Well, the door was open…"

"Yeah, yeah, come in," she grumbled. "Don't stand there holding up the window."

"Sorry." He carefully maneuvered through the room and set the glass against the wall next to the boarded-up bay window. "As I was saying, I can help you get where you're going faster. My bike is parked outside."

"Bike?" Val asked skeptically. "Are you going to put me on your handlebars?"

Gunter's booming laugh filled the living room.

"No, not my bicycle. My motorcycle. I'd be happy to give you a ride."

"You have a motorcycle?" Val perked up. She'd been missing the Ural something fierce.

"Yup. She's a vintage BMW. Got her parked out front. The sidecar is full of glass right now, but give me a few minutes to bring it in, and we should be good to go."

"You even have a sidecar?" Val asked incredulously. "If I didn't know better, I'd say the gods are smiling on us today."

"Maybe they are," Rosa said. "The gods work in mysterious ways."

A short time later, Val found herself straddling the seat of Gunter's motorcycle, the big troll balanced like a mountain in front of her. Rosa huddled in the sidecar. The BMW was in perfect shape, the chassis and tailpipes gleaming.

"How long have you had her?" Val shouted over the wind and engine noise. The BMW was quieter than the Ural, but she was still a healthy bike and put out an equally healthy amount of noise.

"I picked her up about six months ago. She was in pretty sad shape. I like fixing old bikes up," Gunter shouted back over his shoulder.

"Bikes plural? Do you have a collection?"

"Nah, I just fix them up and sell them. I'm not into collecting things, it's the restoration that appeals to me. I like making broken things beautiful again. Like your apartment." The troll laughed — a big booming sound that Val could feel through her hands on his ribcage. It was weird sitting passenger on a bike, but she had to admit that the huge troll made an excellent windbreak.

"Lucky for us," Val called back.

They roared over the pass and out into the western part of the city. The sun had already dipped below the horizon and the final lingering rays dabbed the clouds with gold far out over the Pacific. Gunter swerved to the curb a block away from the cave and the motorcycle rumbled to a stop. As he killed the engine, the sudden silence felt even louder than the BMW.

"Thanks for the lift," Val said as she and Rosa clambered onto the sidewalk.

Gunter got off the bike as well, then reached down into the sidecar and pulled out a massive wrench as long as Val's forearm.

"What's that for?" Val asked.

The troll exposed his blocky teeth in a wide grin.

"Protection, of course. I'm going with you."

"No, you're not. You said you'd give us a ride and you did. We can take it from here."

"Maybe they've beefed up security since the last time you were out here. Or maybe you could use an extra hand carrying stuff." The troll shrugged one shoulder. "Either way, it never hurts to have a big scary troll on your side."

"Gunter, the mayor's involved in this. We could get arrested. I can't ask you to do that."

Gunter's grin widened. "Then it's a good thing you didn't ask, isn't it?"

They stared at each other for a long moment.

"You're just going to follow along no matter what I say, aren't you?" Val sighed.

The big troll laughed. "You hit the nail on the head."

"Fine. I guess you're big enough to make your own decisions. Just do me a favor and don't get shot or anything, OK?"

Gunter saluted her with his wrench. "Aye, aye, captain."

They covered the last block on foot, slowing as they neared the fenced-off site. Bright floodlights illuminated the area. Val was thankful for the deepening gloom as they crept forward on the sidewalk.

"Follow my lead," she whispered. "Don't do anything stupid and let me handle the guards."

As they got closer, they could see that something was happening at the site. There was a white van parked in front of the lot, with people in white coats moving in and out of a dark maw — the cave entrance.

"This is not ideal." Val cursed as they crouched behind a car and watched the people coming and going.

"Stealth does seem to be out of the question," Gunter agreed. "Good thing you brought a big ugly troll. We don't do stealth anyway."

"Something is coming out," Rosa whispered.

Two people pushing a gurney emerged into the floodlights. It was slow going as they struggled to wrestle the wheels of the gurney over the uneven ground of the construction site. The gurney was covered in a white sheet with a body-shaped lump beneath it.

"That's Jorge," Rosa hissed. She started to rise to her feet, but Val put a restraining hand on her arm.

"Hold on, we can't just walk in there and demand they give his body to us. That's a surefire way to get arrested again."

"We cannot let them take him," Rosa insisted, her eyes burning with righteous fervor.

"We won't. But we need to be smart about it."

"No, that's my nephew. His body belongs to his family. I am done waiting." Rosa shook off Val's hand and stalked toward the floodlights.

Val grimaced and eyed the guards. There were at least three that she could see holding guns. Possibly more inside the cave or the guardhouse. The moment Rosa stepped into the light, all those weapons would be pointed directly at her.

# 41

Val gathered her power. The second Rosa stepped into the light, things could get out of hand fast. She had to be ready to protect her friend. She stood poised, skin tingling with power, ready to create a distraction. To call down the power of the storm and give the guards something else to worry about other than putting bullets into Rosa.

Except she never got the chance.

Rosa was two steps away from the floodlights when the barometric pressure plummeted so rapidly that Val felt her ears pop. Dark clouds swirled above the construction site, boiling up out of nowhere. Flashbulb lightning turned the world white. Thunder made the guards cower. Rain hammered down.

As Val's flash-blinded eyes slowly adjusted, she saw a dark shape materialize beside the gurney. A figure in a long dark coat, face shrouded beneath the brim of his fedora. The Rain King.

The guards shouted at him, raising their weapons. The Rain King ignored them, the downpour getting harder as he lifted his hand. The people pushing the gurney fell to their knees, clutching their throats.

The guards opened fire.

The Rain King didn't flinch, bullets disappearing into the dark void of his coat like so many drops of water. He flicked a hand toward the guards and the rain intensified around them, thickening until their shapes were a watery blur. They fell to their knees, clutching their throats.

"Hey! Knock it off," Val shouted as she stepped into the light.

She punched out at him with a fist of wind, hoping to at least draw the Rain King's attention away from the guards. Not that she thought the guards were good people, but still. Nobody deserved to die like that.

The temperature dropped several degrees as the Rain King's attention shifted to her. Val shivered.

"You interfere with my mission again." His voice was the low rumble of distant thunder.

"If your mission is drowning more people, then, yes, I'm interfering."

"These people deserve to die."

"Do they? And you get to decide that? No. I don't know who you think appointed you judge, jury and executioner, but you're wrong."

"You know nothing about this. This is not your business."

"I'm making it my business."

The Rain King shrugged, the barest lifting of his shoulders.

"If that is your choice, you may die with them."

Rain poured down on Val, a deluge so heavy it drove her to her knees. Water covered her mouth and nose, flowing down her throat and into her lungs. Her body spasmed and coughed as she tried to breath, but she only sucked in more water. She tried to push it away with air, to create a bubble around her face. The water was too heavy, clinging stubbornly to her skin. The Rain King wasn't going to let her use the same trick this time.

Her body spasmed, lungs burning as they fought desperately for air. Sharp pain filled her chest.

She punched out with the wind, but it only made the Rain King's coat flap. The water didn't let up. Her vision started to dim.

She needed air. Needed to breathe.

In desperation, she reached out to the storm. Felt the churning clouds crackling with electricity. She called it to her, gathered it and, as everything faded to black around her, hurled it at the Rain King.

The world exploded as a thick bolt of lightning lanced down on the Rain King's head. White light seared Val's retinas, destroying the darkness in an instant. The roar of the thunder pummeled down in waves, driving away all thought and sensation.

The Rain King convulsed in the current, suspended like a marionette for an endless moment. Then the bolt cut out as quickly as it had appeared and he staggered, his dark form smoking as he collapsed to one knee.

The water fell away from Val's face and she sucked in the sweetest breath she'd ever taken.

They both knelt there, panting like a pair of prize fighters, down but not out, slowly gathering the strength to go another round. In a perfectly synchronized movement, they staggered to their feet, eyes locked on one another. Val drew a deep breath, clenched her fists, set her jaw, and prepared for battle.

Rosa's voice rang out as she stepped into the light.

"Jorge! Stop this right now!"

All eyes turned toward the seer. Rosa's scarf flapped in the howling wind, her emaciated body swaying like a willow branch. But she remained upright, bending but not breaking. Her eyes blazed like twin volcanoes.

It took Val a moment to realize what she had just said.

Jorge?

She turned to stare at the Rain King. But he was looking at her no longer. All his attention was focused on Rosa. Though his face was hidden beneath the shadow of a hat, Val could feel the dark pulse of his attention. His eyes were pools of even deeper darkness. Black holes sucking all light from the galaxy.

His voice cracked. *"Tía?"*

Rosa nodded, her eyes filling with tears.

"What have they done to you, *mi hijo*?"

The rain stopped as abruptly as if someone had twisted the tap. The wind stopped howling. The entire world held its breath as the Rain King took a hesitant step forward. Then another.

He stopped two steps away from Rosa and shook his head. He drew himself up.

"No. Jorge is dead. All that remains is the Rain King." His voice was as cold as the Pacific wind.

Rosa said nothing. She simply stepped forward and embraced him.

## 42

"Such a touching scene. Someone should make a lifetime movie out of it." Mayor Light's aid, Roland, stepped forward into the floodlight glare. The harsh light cast his face into planes of light and shadow. However, the gray man's tone was as bland as ever, his suit and hair aggressively nondescript.

Val's hackles rose. "What have you done?"

"What needed to be done," he replied. "That's my job. I do what needs to be done, so the mayor doesn't have to."

"So you're a fixer?"

"Labels mean little to me. Call me what you like." A not-quite smile thinned Roland's lips. "I will do my job regardless."

"And your job is what? Sacrificing people? Creating monsters?"

"My job," he said, stressing the word, "is to make sure the mayor's agenda advances. Governing a city is like maintaining a fleet of vehicles. Keeping things running smoothly requires constant maintenance and vigilance. There are a thousand little details you have to stay on top of: tire pressure, oil changes, tune ups. Not to mention repairs when things do not go as planned."

"So you are a fixer."

"Perhaps. You could call me the Mechanic, if you like. When unexpected problems arise, I'm the one who gets my hands dirty."

"Dirty? Or bloody?"

"Whatever the situation requires."

The thin not-smile reappeared. Val shuddered. She had the feeling the man enjoyed getting his hands dirty.

"So why this?" she asked, gesturing to Jorge's covered body on the gurney. "Ritual sacrifice seems like an extreme step."

"There are forces awakening in this city. Forces even the mayor needs some help handling. Creatures out of nightmare. Werewolves and goblins. Witches and vampires. The mayor needs soldiers to combat these forces. To keep his people safe." He gestured to the Rain King. "Behold our avenging angel."

"Jorge does not belong to you," Rosa hissed.

"Quite right," the Mechanic said smoothly. "He does not. He belongs to the city. As I said, he is a tool. I am but the humble hand that wields it."

"It seems you don't know how to control your tool very well," Val snapped. "The last time I saw him, he was drowning your supporters in the Mission Shifter Settlement riot."

"As a tool he can be imprecise," he acknowledged. "But you neglect to mention that he also drowned a great many shifters as well. Doing God's work, some might say. A bit of collateral damage is to be expected."

The Rain King echoed Rosa's words. "I do not belong to you."

"Not to me, no. I am simply the middleman. A humble pawn in the trenches, making sure the important things get done. Middle management at its finest. Nevertheless, you will follow my orders. We all have our place in the pecking order."

"You cannot compel me." The Rain King swelled like a thunderhead, eyes flashing. "I am a force of nature."

"Compel you? I wouldn't dream of it. I'm a manager, not a slave driver. Cooperation is the key to keeping any organization running smoothly. We believe in perks and incentives. You should see our Friday pizza party spread."

"He's coming with us," Val said. "And we're taking Jorge's body. Don't try to stop us."

She drew in her power and held it, ready to fight. She had no idea what the man was capable of, but she knew he must be hiding something beneath that bland exterior.

"I'm sorry you feel that way." The Mechanic smiled. "Kill them."

The guards opened fire.

As the first shots exploded into the night, Val yanked the air sideways. Would a shield of wind stop bullets? She didn't know, but she was about to find out.

Pain seared through her bicep, the force of the bullet nearly spinning her around. She cursed. It turned out the answer was no.

As a second guard turned his barrel in her direction, she desperately swung the wind down along the excavated ground, scooping up dirt and gravel, flinging it at the gunmen's eyes. Too slow. The muzzle flashed as the guard squeezed the trigger.

Then a wall of flesh was standing between her and the gunman. Gunter grunted as several bullets sank into his body. To the side, she saw the Rain King shielding Rosa in the same way.

She heard the gunman exclaim, their shots becoming erratic as her blown grit finally did its job. But it was too late for Gunter. The big troll staggered and fell to one knee, blood soaking his shirt.

"Gunter!" Val reached for him… only to jerk her hand back in surprise as he lurched back to his feet. He turned his big, square-toothed grin on her.

"No worries. Trolls regenerate." He stuck a finger into one of the holes in his stomach and fished around for a moment before emerging with a bloody lump clutched between his fingers. He grimaced and flicked the bullet onto the ground. "Still hurts like a bitch, though."

He rolled his shoulders and hefted his wrench before advancing on the blinded gunmen.

"Now for some payback."

"I think that's enough," the lady in pink stepped into the clearing, her soft voice pouring over them like honey. "There's no need for violence."

A tidal wave of sensation rolled over Val.

The rich scent of a blooming field of wildflowers on a spring day. Small birds singing in the trees.

A warm breeze across her cheeks. Soft fingers caressing her hair. The taste of strawberries.

The woman smiled and it was more lovely than a hundred sunrises.

She walked over to the Rain King and took his hand.

"Come along now," she cooed, her voice a symphony of one. "We have work to do."

She tugged gently and the Rain King followed her toward the darkness, meek as a lamb on a rope. At the edge of the light, she paused and looked back over her shoulder at Val, Rosa, and Gunter.

"I think you'd better stay here for a while. Enjoy the night air."

She led the Rain King away and they were swallowed by the darkness.

Val's world remained a hazy blur of impressions. An intoxicating swirl of scents and sounds. Rose petals brushing against her skin. Sensations so overwhelming they became a waking dream. Beauty and wonder she could taste. The air moving in and out of her lungs was honeyed syrup. Time lost all meaning.

When she finally came back to herself, a peach dawn was brushing the sky. The woman in pink was gone, and she had taken the Rain King, the Mechanic, Jorge's body, and everything else with her. The construction site around her was dark and empty. Even the fencing was gone.

Val groaned. Her muscles were stiff and sore and she was shivering. Had she been standing in one place all night?

Beside her, she heard an answering moan. Rubbing her stiff neck, she turned and saw Gunter and Rosa lying on the ground.

"Who the hell was that?" Gunter sat up, rubbing at his shaggy head. "What did she do to us?"

"She works for the mayor," Val said. Her voice was scratchy, her throat dry. "Or maybe he works for her."

"She took Jorge. We have to stop her," Rosa said.

"Yeah." The memory of rose petals brushed soft against Val's mind. She shivered. "Something tells that might be easier said than done."

## 43

"Now you're fighting the mayor's office? You do know there's nothing wrong with picking battles you can actually win, right?" Malcolm clucked disapprovingly as he whirled about the kitchen, slinging pots and pans. Val had no idea what he was making, but so many bottles and bowls were involved that he might have taken up a new career as a mad scientist.

"I don't pick the fights, Malcolm. They pick me." Val sighed into her butterscotch coffee. She and Rosa sat at the small table in the kitchen while Gunter banged about installing windows in the living room.

"On the bright side, at least we know who the Rain King is now," Gunter called out. The troll showed no ill effects from being shot several times and was just as cheerful as ever. He was literally whistling while he worked.

Val wanted to strangle him.

"Is that a bright side? Rosa's nephew has been turned into some kind of rain god. I don't think I'd call that a positive development."

"Well, it's better than him being dead, right?" Malcolm interjected.

Val grunted. "I'm still unclear on that, actually. We saw his body, but Rosa's visions say he's not dead. I have no idea how that works."

"Jorge has been reborn. One flesh exchanged for another," Rosa said, her tone ominous as the tolling of a bell.

Malcolm gave her the side-eye.

"You know, you could just tell us what's happening in a normal human being voice. You don't have to be so dramatic."

"Not be dramatic? This from the drama queen herself?" Val gave Malcolm the side-eye right back.

He was unfazed. "Yes, but that is my natural state. It doesn't suit Rosa. She's usually a lot more practical than this."

"He must be freed from his chains," Rosa said, her eyes black pits containing universes. "What was taken must be returned by the time of the full moon. If we do not restore the balance, the streets will run with blood."

"What was taken?" Val asked. "What does that mean?"

"I don't know, but the streets running with blood sounds a lot different to me now that I'm a vampire." Malcolm cocked his head. "Damn. Now I'm hungry."

Rosa ran a hand over her face.

"I'm sorry, I… It's getting hard to separate the visions from reality. I feel like I'm moving through a waking dream. Everywhere I look, there are signs and portents. I can't tell what's real anymore." For a moment, the old Rosa was back, and she looked terrified.

Val wanted to reassure her. Reach out and take her hand. She did not.

"We'll figure it out," she said instead, trying to project a confidence she didn't feel. "We'll get back what was taken. Save Jorge and restore the balance."

"What is this thing that we need to get back?" Malcolm asked.

"I don't know."

They both looked at Rosa expectantly.

Val could see the struggle in her friend's face. The seer and the woman at war within one flesh. It hurt her to see how gaunt Rosa had become. Her skin was pale and waxy, stretched tight over her skull. Her sunken eyes were bruised pits. She looked like she hadn't slept in weeks.

"There's a totem?" Rosa said uncertainly. "It's hard to see. When I try to focus on it, it's blurred, wavering like an object underwater. I think it might be a staff. It's covered with native runes carved into the stone."

"Stone?" Val asked. "The staff is made of stone? Not wood?"

"It is stone," Rosa confirmed. "I think it was ceremonial."

"I certainly hope so," Malcolm put in. "Can you imagine hitting someone with a stone staff? Or even just carrying around something that heavy? My back hurts just thinking about it."

"Do you have any idea where this staff is?" Val asked. "Or where it needs to be returned to?"

"I don't know where it is," Rosa said. "But Jorge does. As the Rain King, it's connected to him. I think it might be helping the mayor's people control him. If we can get the staff back, we will free Jorge."

Val chewed her bottom lip. "OK, that's useful information. Where does the staff need to be returned to?"

"The chamber where we found Jorge's body," Rosa said immediately. "There's a slot on the altar where the staff is supposed to lie."

"Well, we've got half the puzzle. Now we just need to figure out where the staff is and get it back to its rightful place," Malcolm chirped.

"And we need to avoid the woman in pink while we're at it," Val said sourly. "Whatever mind-control mojo she's got really put a whammy on us all."

"What do you think she is?" Malcolm asked.

*"She is a succubus,"* Mister E said in Val's mind. *"And a powerful one. She uses her seductive powers to charm you so thoroughly that she wipes all other thoughts right out of your head."*

"She's a succubus?" Val asked. "Does that mean she wants to have sex with us?"

She didn't realize she'd spoken aloud until Malcolm said, "Sex with all of us? As in, an orgy with this group? We could have a real live monster mash."

Val groaned as Malcolm started to sing.

*"No, that does not mean she wants to have sex with all of you. Or any of you,"* Mister E corrected. *"She's powerful enough to be able to use her powers to seduce you into doing what she wants without any bodily fluids*

*being swapped. Though if she does decide to get physical, watch out. If she can spin your head so easily without any physical contact, I'd hate to see what she can do with skin-on-skin."*

Val relayed the spirit-cat's analysis to the others.

Malcolm pouted. "Awww, I really wanted to do the monster mash."

"You're a vampire, Malcolm. Anytime you mash, it's a monster mash."

"You're right, it is." He brightened and went back to whatever he was concocting, singing happily.

Val sighed.

"OK. According to Rosa's vision, we need to get the staff back in place before the full moon rises. Unfortunately, that's tonight. So where can we find this staff, and how do we get it back?"

"I can help with the first part, at least." Rosa leaned forward. "I know where the mayor is keeping the staff."

"Great, that makes our job easy," Val said.

"No, it doesn't. He's keeping the staff in City Hall."

Val groaned and rubbed her suddenly aching temples.

# 44

"All we have to do is break into City Hall? Piece of cake." Malcolm grinned.

He, Val, Rosa, and Gunter were crouched behind a parked car across the street from the grand gold-domed building. A pale light crept around the edges of the skyscrapers to the east as the moon slowly woke from her slumber.

"Famous last words," Val grumbled.

She didn't like the plan they'd come up with, but she didn't have a better one. And they were out of time. They needed to get the staff back now, before it was too late.

At least it was after hours and, as far as they could tell, City Hall was deserted. Still, attempting to break into the mayor's office seemed like a recipe for disaster.

"You're sure the staff is in his office?" she asked Rosa for perhaps the dozenth time.

"Yes," the seer snapped.

Fair enough. If someone kept asking Val the same question over and over, she'd be a little short tempered too.

They avoided the guard at the well-lit main entrance and circled around the side of the building, staying in the shadows as much as possible. The side entrance was quiet, lit by only a single bulb above the door, and appeared unguarded.

"I thought there would be more security," Malcolm said.

"What for?" Gunter asked. "It's not like they have vaults of gold in there. It's just offices and paperwork."

"Sure, but the way they carry on about how important that paperwork is, you would think they'd want to keep it more secure."

"One person's trash is another person's treasure."

Malcolm stared at him.

"And your point is?"

"We all value different things." The big troll shrugged.

"And I value getting into this building undetected. So if you could both shut up, that'd be great," Val hissed, scowling at the doorway. "I wish I had a way to take out that lightbulb."

Two seconds later, the lightbulb popped, broken glass tinkling down in front of the doorway.

Val flinched. "What the hell was that?"

"Low-tech solution. I hit it with a rock," Gunter said.

"Did you miss the part where we're trying to be quiet?"

"You said you wanted the light out. It's out." The troll grinned, impervious to her ire.

Val ground her teeth and watched the doorway. When no alarm sounded, she let out a relieved breath.

"It looks like your solution worked. Lucky for you. If you'd screwed up this entire mission before it even got started, I'd have made rocky mountain oysters out of troll."

Gunter's face scrunched. "What are rocky mountain oysters?"

"Trust me, you do not want to know," Malcolm cut in. "This is definitely one of those times where ignorance is bliss."

Gunter shrugged and dropped it.

They slipped up to the now dark entrance, keeping an eye out for guards on patrol, either inside or outside the building. The door itself was sturdy, but the lock was simple enough. Val froze the mechanism and Gunter shattered the lock with a single hammer and chisel blow.

The hallway inside was dim, lit only by the red glow of an emergency exit sign over the door.

"Any idea where the mayor's office is?" Gunter whispered.

"According to the blueprints Malcolm got, it's upstairs on the second floor," Val said.

"Blueprints?" Gunter raised an eyebrow.

"I've got friends in high places." Malcolm smiled. "And low places. I've got friends everywhere, really."

They moved through the dark building, pausing twice to let patrolling security guards pass by. Every footstep sounded like a gunshot in the deserted hallways. Val found herself holding her breath as they crept up the stairs to the second floor. Finally, they stood outside the door to the mayor's office.

Val raised her hands, preparing to freeze the lock once again.

"Wait," Rosa hissed. She reached out and tried the knob. To Val's astonishment, it turned. Rosa smiled. "Always try the easy way first."

The office was small, with a couple of leather chairs and a small desk off to one side.

"I expected the mayor's office to be bigger," Gunter said.

"It is. This is the receptionists' area." Malcolm opened a door behind the small desk. "This is the mayor's office."

The room he revealed was four times the size of the reception area. The mayor's office was dominated by an oak desk the size of a pool table. Bookshelves full of law books covered the wall behind it.

"Somebody's compensating for something." Malcolm smirked.

"Do you think Mayor Light has read all of these books?" Rosa asked.

"I'd be shocked if he's read any of them," Val replied.

"How do you think they got this desk in here?" Malcolm wondered. "It's too big to fit through the door."

"They probably brought it in through the windows," Gunter said confidently. "They do that a lot in some cities, especially old ones. Have you ever seen pictures of Amsterdam? They've got hooks on the front of every building for hauling furniture up from the street."

They all stood there for a minute, looking back and forth from the desk to the oversized windows, trying to picture the operation.

Val shook her head. "We're getting distracted. Where's the staff?"

"Right here." Rosa reached up and pulled a rune-covered staff from a display on the wall. She promptly dropped it, the stone *thunking* loudly against the polished wooden floor. She grimaced. "Sorry. It's a lot heavier than it looks."

Val tried to pick it up and shook her head. "You aren't kidding. It's a good thing we brought a troll with us. Gunter, will you do the honors?"

Gunter grinned and lifted the staff with one hand.

"Nice biceps." Malcolm squeezed the muscles in question, smirking as the big troll flushed.

"Let's get out of here." Val led the way back to the hall and down the stairs. As they slipped out the side door and into the plaza, she said, "We need to get this staff back to the altar before moonrise. How much time do we have?"

"One hour," Rosa answered.

"That should be plenty of time, assuming we don't run into any trouble between here and there."

"Assumptions are dangerous," a new voice said behind them.

They whirled to find the Mechanic stepping out of the darkness.

# 45

"How are you going to stop us? I'm not tied to a chair this time," Val snarled.

"Me?" Surprise flitted across the Mechanic's face, before his features returned to their customary bland expression. "I'm not stopping anyone. I'm an administrator, not a fighter."

"Perfect. If you know what's good for you, you'll stay the hell out of our way."

"My associates, on the other hand, are definitely fighters," the Mechanic continued. A horde of squat, dark shapes came pouring around the corner of the building, green fingers clutching spears and wicked spiked clubs. Pale moonlight gleamed on teeth and knives, making their yellow eyes shine.

"Goblins?" Val said. "But the mayor evicted them from their homes. Why would they fight for you?"

The Mechanic smiled.

"Goblins are warriors, first and foremost. Like all mercenaries throughout the ages, they don't really care who they fight for, so long as they get paid."

Val eyed the squat horde warily. She'd gotten a taste of how dangerous goblin warriors could be at the zoo. Goblins were short, but powerful. They were also sneaky, working as a group to surround and overwhelm their prey with numbers. And they definitely had numbers here. Val counted a couple dozen goblins, at least.

To say nothing of the lions.

What looked to be an entire pride of lions stalked among the goblins. They looked huge standing shoulder-to-shoulder with the goblins. Also, they were doing something Val hadn't seen the last time she'd encountered them.

"Goblins riding lions?" Malcolm asked. "Isn't that a little over the top?"

The Mechanic held out his hand.

"Give me the staff and no one gets hurt. We can all walk away friends."

"We will never be friends," Val snarled.

"You have no idea how much it saddens me to hear that." The Mechanic made an exaggerated frown, then turned to the goblins. "You know what to do."

The goblins bared their teeth.

"Don't do this," Val called out to them. "That man is the real enemy here. He and his boss are human-first bigots who hate supernaturals. They run persecution campaigns against shifters and magical creatures of every type. They organize mobs who attack and kill supernatural refugees. Why would you work for people like that? You should be helping us, not fighting us."

"What color is your gold?" A female goblin astride a lion asked. She nudged it with her heels, and the animal stalked forward from the mob. The goblin hooked a thumb under a necklace dangling over her collarbone, lifting it so the metal caught the light and shone. "His is gold-colored."

The goblin looked familiar. Val frowned, then she remembered. It was the female goblin who had first captured her and taken her to the queen. The hostile one who had argued against helping her.

She sighed. Why couldn't anything ever be easy?

"Is that all you care about? Gold?" she asked. "You'll fight for people who hate you? Who would gladly slaughter every one of you. Just for some shiny metal?"

The goblin laughed.

"Is that a question? You don't know goblins very well, do you? Gold comes first. Everything else comes second. Also"—a dangerous glint came into her eye—"I remember you, witch. I wanted to kill you the last time I saw you. The queen wouldn't let me. Now your blood is mine."

"Hand over the staff," the Mechanic said. "This is your final warning."

"Rosa," Val whispered. "Get ready to run."

"Run where?" Rosa asked. "I'm not going to outrun lions."

"You won't have to." Val stepped to the side to put her body between the seer and the goblins. "Malcolm, Gunter, let's keep Rosa behind us."

Malcolm looked at the goblin horde doubtfully.

"I mean, we can try, but that's a lot of goblins. I don't think they're going to stand in a line and let us fight them one at a time."

"Do you have a better idea?"

"We could run?"

"Did you miss the part about the lions?"

"Well, I could run. Vampires are fast. I'm just saying…" He trailed off under Val's glare before sighing dramatically. "Having mortal friends is so inconvenient sometimes."

"Just shut up and do your best to keep Rosa protected," Val snapped.

"Aye aye, Captain." Malcolm gave her a mock salute.

Val ignored it, focusing on drawing up her power.

"You're not going to hand it over? A pity. We could have avoided all of this." The Mechanic sounded bored. He turned to the goblins and flicked his fingers in their direction.

With a great war cry, the goblin horde surged forward.

Val called up a gale, yanking the cold wind out of the sky. It swept along the plaza, gathering dust and debris, before she drove the cloud directly into their attackers' faces. The goblins coughed, spat and raised hands to shield their eyes. The lions yowled, fur bristling as they turned their backs to the wind.

"Hit them now!" she shouted.

Gunter waded into the mass of goblins, towering over the little green warriors like a giant. Most of them only came up to his waist. He held the staff in one hand and a massive wrench in the other. He raised the wrench and hesitated, looking down at the little creatures coughing and spitting before him.

"It doesn't seem fair," he called back. "They can't even see me."

"It's a street fight, Gunter, not a boxing match. It's not supposed to be fair. There are also a lot more of them than there are of us. Do you think that's fair?"

"No. But still… Ow!" His objection turned to a curse as one of the goblins jabbed him in the leg with a spear. "That's it, you little shit."

Gunter hit the goblin over the head with his massive fist. It went down, but another lunged forward to take its place. Within seconds, Gunter was surrounded, hewing and kicking at the little warriors like a modern-day Gulliver. They surrounded him, stabbing and clubbing at his legs.

Val cursed. Despite his size, Gunter was already bleeding from a half dozen wounds. He was going to be overwhelmed by the goblin horde's numbers. And he was the one carrying the staff, which meant most of the goblins were swarming around him, ignoring the rest of them completely.

"I think we made a tactical error," she called out to Malcolm. "Can you get the staff from Gunter?"

"I don't know," Malcolm said doubtfully. "That's a lot of goblins. With a lot of spears. Don't you want me to stay back here and protect Rosa?"

"Are they attacking Rosa? Or are they going after the staff?"

"Why don't you go get it? You're the great and powerful Val Keri!"

"Because I can't carry the damn thing! It's made of stone!"

"Fine, I'll get it." But Malcolm stayed frozen to the spot, eyes wide as he watched the goblins ebb and swirl around Gunter like waves in a very dangerous sea.

Val ground her teeth. She supposed she shouldn't be surprised. Vampire powers or no, Malcolm wasn't a fighter.

"Just grab the spear," she barked. "I'll clear a path for you."

How to do that was a mystery. Any burst of wind she threw at the goblins would hit Gunter as well. She could call down lightning, but that was even more iffy. Electricity tended to jump from body to body in a crowd, and she had no control over which bodies it would jump to. Lightning would be as likely to zap Gunter as the goblins.

There was no avoiding it. She was going to have to get her hands dirty.

"Fine." Val huffed and waded into the melee.

# 46

**P**unching things was fun. At least, Val had always thought so. Sparring at the gym was her go-to workout. It was a great way to release stress and endorphins. And it was amazing full-body exercise, cardio and muscle toning all in one.

She hadn't been getting to the gym as much as she would have liked lately. Too busy tracking down monsters and missing persons.

So part of her was pleased to have the chance to punch something. Or someone. Many someones, actually.

She waded into the mass of goblins, laying about left and right, her fists connecting with green faces as she tried to clear a path to Gunter. She jabbed a goblin in the eye with a left. Elbowed another one in the temple before cracking a third across the jaw with a short roundhouse. The goblins were focused on Gunter and the staff, so for several seconds Val was able to stride through the crowd unnoticed, knocking goblins aside like plastic dolls.

It was all great fun, until the squat warriors started trying to stab her.

That was something Val had failed to consider. When she sparred with someone, they generally didn't respond by trying to bury pointy things in her flesh.

She twisted to avoid a knife thrust to her stomach, hissing as a second goblin sliced a spear tip across her thigh instead. She reached down and grabbed the shaft of the spear, pulling the goblin forward and planting her fist in its surprised little face as she wrenched the weapon away from it.

She hefted the spear in satisfaction, fingers curling around the rough wooden shaft. That was better. You had to fight fire with fire. Or, you know, spears with spears.

Her time to enjoy her victory was all too brief. Two more goblins came at her with pointy things, one clutching a long knife and the other armed with yet another spear.

Val didn't know much about spears. They weren't a weapon you generally found in modern gyms. She growled in frustration as she jabbed ineffectually with the tip. The goblin easily knocked it aside, forcing her to retreat. Then the little warrior stabbed her with its spear in return and she twisted, blocking the thrust with the shaft of her spear.

Inspiration struck.

She might not have ever fought with a spear, but she had trained with a quarterstaff plenty of times. And wasn't a spear just a quarterstaff with a blade attached to one end? She adjusted her grip, holding the spear shaft across her body like a staff, ignoring the tip.

The goblin with the knife lunged in, slashing at her stomach. Val swung the end of the spear down in a block, cracking the little creature on the wrist. The knife clattered to the ground, the goblin crying out as tiny bones shattered.

The spear-wielder tried to take advantage of her distraction with a thrust, but Val took a step back and pivoted, pushing the center of the vertical shaft across to knock the tip offline. It missed her midriff by inches. She then whipped the butt end of the shaft up into the goblin's groin. Apparently goblins didn't like that move any more than humans did. Her assailant collapsed with a groan.

Val grinned. That was the nice thing about the quarterstaff — or the spear, in this case. The shaft had two ends, allowing you to transition from offense to defense in an instant. Block with one end, then whip the other end around to attack. It was an elegant, balanced weapon, and Val had always enjoyed sparring with it.

This was going to be fun after all.

She started to move forward again, cracking goblins with the shaft of the spear, bruising and breaking bones with every swing. She got lost in the rhythm of the fight. Move, block, strike, repeat. Body and mind acting as one.

Val was enjoying herself so much that she was momentarily confused when she heard Gunter cry out. Lost in the swirl of violence, riding her adrenaline high, she had forgotten all about the troll, and had nearly forgotten the reason they were fighting.

She turned and saw the big troll go down, disappearing beneath a wave of goblins. Cursing, Val tried to fight her way in that direction, pushing and striking out at every goblin in her path. But there were too many of them. Every step took painful seconds. Seconds Gunter might not have.

She ground her teeth. Desperate times called for desperate measures.

Val reached deep, calling for her power.

She felt Mister E stir with grin.

*"I thought you'd never ask."*

Power surged through her, exploding outward in a roaring hundred-mile-per-hour wind. A wave of goblins was flattened, clearing the way between where she stood and the spot where she'd seen Gunter go down. She spotted the troll now, his bulky body sprawled on the ground amid the downed goblins. He wasn't moving.

Val stumbled forward over her flattened foes, shaking with fear and rage. Gunter couldn't be dead. She couldn't lose another friend.

A few goblins raised their heads and tried to grab her legs as she walked over them. She obligingly kicked them in the face with her boot.

Reaching the spot where Gunter lay, she was relieved to see the big troll was still breathing. But her own breath caught when she saw how much blood stained his shirt and pants. He'd been punctured dozens of times by the goblins' spears and knives.

Val tried to find the worst wounds, tried to put pressure on them to stop the bleeding. Yet there were so many. Each wound might be small, but they added up. She knew that trolls were famously hard to kill due to their innate regeneration, but could even Gunter's healing powers save him from this? Val was neither a doctor nor an expert on troll physiology. All she could do was keep him from getting stabbed more, and hope it was enough.

"Val!" Malcolm's cry pulled her from her thoughts.

She swiveled her head to see the vampire waving frantically. It took her a second, but then she saw what he was worked up about. Val cursed. A group of goblins were running off with the stone staff.

## 47

Val hesitated, her gaze swiveling from the fleeing goblins to the unconscious Gunter and back again. Her hands were stained red with the troll's blood as she tried to keep pressure on the worst of his wounds. She couldn't let him to bleed to death.

"Stop them!" she called out to Malcolm.

"How?" Malcolm wrung his hands.

"You're a vampire! You're ridiculously fast and strong. Use your powers!"

Malcolm wavered.

She watched him make a decision. His hands curled into fists as he gathered himself. Then he took a deep breath, grimaced, and charged after the goblins.

Malcolm blurred across the asphalt, catching the fleeing goblins in the blink of an eye. He went straight to the staff, grabbing it and trying to wrench it away from them with his vampire strength. It almost worked as the goblins carrying the staff were yanked off their feet.

Unfortunately, the staff was incredibly heavy, and a half dozen goblins had been working together to carry it. Had only one or two goblins been carrying the staff, Malcolm would have torn it out of their grip in an instant. But six was too many. He did manage to stop their forward momentum, causing the whole group to lurch to the side as he grabbed hold of the staff and pulled, but he did not tear it away. The goblins hung on, six pairs of hands grimly vying against the strength of one vampire.

An awkward tug of war ensued, with Malcolm yanking on the staff and the goblins refusing to let go. He dragged them across the paving stones of the plaza, the goblins bumping along like tin cans tied to a newlywed's back bumper. But he couldn't shake them. As she watched, three more goblins joined the fray, one grabbing hold of the staff while the other two threw themselves at Malcolm, wrapping their little arms around his legs. He tried to kick them off, but they clung like stubborn barnacles.

"Val," he called out. "A little help?"

She looked from Malcolm to Gunter. The troll's wounds seemed to be bleeding less, his regeneration closing the worst of them. She thought he might be out of the danger zone, but she wasn't sure. Maybe she could stop putting pressure on his gashes and leave him to heal on his own. Maybe.

Another yelp from Malcolm drew her attention back across the plaza. Several more goblins had joined the fray, surrounding him and poking at him with spears. It looked like his vampire speed was allowing him to avoid being impaled by the attacks, but with the pair of goblins weighing his legs down and his hands gripping the staff, he was forced into an awkward set of gyrations, leaning first one way then the other to avoid the jabbing spears. It was as if he were playing a bizarre game of Goblin Twister.

More goblins kept adding their bodies to the fray. Val cursed. No matter how fast Malcolm was, he couldn't dance around those spear tips forever. Eventually, the goblin's numbers would overwhelm him, just as they had Gunter.

But could she leave the wounded troll?

Rosa's voice in her ear solved the dilemma.

"I'll take care of Gunter. Go help Malcolm." The seer knelt and started putting pressure on Gunter's wounds.

Val gave her a startled look, glancing around to make sure there were no goblins ready to run the woman through. There weren't. The little mercenaries were all focused on Malcolm.

"Great. Thank you," she replied.

Rosa just made a shooing motion. "Go, go."

Val didn't need to be told twice.

She sprinted across the plaza, sizing up the situation as she ran. At least two dozen goblins surrounded Malcolm now, and it looked like some of their attacks had finally connected. Dark spots of blood stained Malcolm's shirt. He was slowing down, his movements more and more constricted by the weight of goblins as more squat bodies continued to pile on.

Right. First she had to get the little buggers off him.

Unfortunately, he was in the middle of a crowd, so she was faced with the same problem she'd had trying to help Gunter earlier. There was no way to hit the goblins with her magic without hitting Malcolm as well. It looked like she'd have to wade into the crowd and get her hands dirty again.

That suited her just fine.

She stepped up to the rear of the crowd and swung her spear, knocking aside two goblins who never saw her coming.

"Not very sportsmanlike, but all's fair in love and war," she muttered.

She felled three more before any of them even noticed she was there. Those closest to her raised the alarm and the goblins started turning to face her.

Not fast enough. She poked one of them in the gut, doubling it over, then finished it off with a crack across the temple. Malcolm was only a handful of steps away now. Four more goblins and she'd be at his side.

A snarling roar was her only warning as a mountain of muscle and fur slammed into her back. Val hit the ground, air huffing out of her lungs, face smashing into the paving stones. Long claws raked her left leg. She screamed.

She tried to roll away, but the lion was a lot heavier than she'd expected. Faster too. She ducked her head, trying to protect her face with her arms as the animal's claws raked her body. She thanked her lucky stars for her leather jacket. Without its protection, the big cat would have disemboweled her in seconds.

Val tried to poke the thing with her spear, only to realize the weapon had been knocked from her grasp by the impact. She was unarmed. The lion, in contrast, was heavily armed, with long fangs and wickedly sharp claws.

Right. Magic then.

She punched out with a fist of wind, trying to knock the big cat away. Her blow rocked it back onto its hind legs, but it didn't fly off as she had expected. Her eyes widened. Was the cat that heavy?

Then she saw the reason. The cat wasn't alone. The hostile female goblin crouched atop its back.

She sneered down at Val. "You're not so tough now, are you, witch?"

# 48

Pinned by hundreds of pounds of cat and goblin, unable to wriggle free or push them away with her magic, Val did the only thing she could. She fought dirty.

She yanked her hunting knife out of its sheath and plunged it up into the lion's belly. The big cat roared and leaped off her. Hot blood covered Val's hand as she levered herself onto one elbow. She winced and put her fingers to her bitten thigh. Blood soaked her black jeans.

"Tit for tat," she growled. "You bite me, I bite you."

There was a blur of motion and Malcolm was kneeling at her side.

"Are you all right?" he asked.

"I'm fine." She eyed him suspiciously. "Where's the staff?"

Malcolm couldn't meet her gaze.

"I couldn't get it. There were too many goblins. I'm sorry."

"What?" She whirled in time to see a group of goblins disappearing around the corner of City Hall, staff held triumphantly over their heads. "We have to stop them!"

"We tried, Val. Gunter got stabbed. The goblins got the staff. We failed."

"What part of 'the streets will run with blood' don't you understand? Failure is not an option." Val got to her feet, nearly falling again as she tried to put weight on her wounded leg. Pain knifed through her thigh. She cried out and fell on a discarded spear. Using the shaft as an impromptu crutch, she stubbornly righted herself and started hobbling after the little horde.

"You're in no shape to be chasing anyone," Malcolm said. "You need to bandage that leg before you lose too much blood."

"There's no time, Malcolm," she cried out in frustration as her leg buckled and she nearly fell again. "If we lose that spear, there's no telling where they'll take it. We may never find it again."

"Let me chase them," Malcolm said. "Rosa can bandage your thigh. Maybe I can't get the staff back, but there's no way they're going to outrun me. I can at least track them and report back so we know where the staff is. We can try to get it again when you and Gunter have recovered."

"But we're on a deadline. If we don't return that staff to the burial site by midnight, bad things are going to happen."

"I know. I promise I won't lose it. We've still got a few hours. Get yourself together and you can come after me, OK? Rosa, help me out."

The seer knelt beside Val, already tearing a long scarf into strips to bind her thigh.

"He's right," Rosa said. "Let me bandage your wounds. You can't help anyone in the state you're in."

"Fine. Go," Val snarled. "But don't you dare lose them. Come back as soon as you know where they've gone."

"Aye aye, Captain." Malcolm saluted before turning and dashing off into the night.

Val winced as Rosa wound the scarf around her thigh and cinched it tight.

"How's Gunter?"

"He'll be all right," Rosa said, her dark eyes intent on her work. "Trolls regenerate. He'll be good as new in no time."

"I wish I did that," Val groused.

"Perhaps you made your bargain with the wrong god," Rosa said. "Healing gods are much nicer to deal with than… whatever that thing inside you is."

Val snorted.

"I didn't exactly get multiple gods on the menu to choose from. I got stuck with the only one that was available."

*"I'm right here, you know,"* Mister E complained.

"Well, we all have our crosses to bear." Rosa looked up at her, managing a small smile despite the deep worry lines creasing her forehead as she helped Val to her feet. "That's the best I can do for now. How does that feel?"

The witch winced.

"Like someone stabbed me in the thigh."

Gunter's voice cut in, "Hazards of the job." They whirled to find the big troll striding toward them. "That's what happens when you try to play the hero."

"I don't think you've got any room to talk," Val said wryly. "Didn't you volunteer for this gig? I don't recall asking you to tag along."

"Some people are born to greatness, some have greatness thrust upon them. I can't help it if I get all heroic when I see a friend in need." Gunter shrugged. "Maybe it's a troll thing. It must be in our genes."

"I'm sure that's it." Val rolled her eyes.

"Anyway, what are we all just standing around here for? The bad guys are getting away. Time is wasting!" Gunter took two steps, stopped and looked around in confusion, then took two steps in another direction before stopping again. He scratched his shaggy head. "Which way did they go again?"

"That way," Val pointed. "There's no point in charging off in that direction, though. Malcolm is following them. He's going to come back and tell us where they've gone."

"Or we could follow the white rabbit," Rosa said softly.

"The what?" Val followed the seer's eyes and found a white rabbit sitting near the corner of the building where the goblin horde had disappeared. The rabbit's fur shone like moonlight.

"It seems you have earned the favor of the Moon Goddess," Rosa said. "That is her companion."

Now Val stared at Rosa.

"Yes, it is. But how do you know that?"

Rosa's smile became a smirk.

"There are some perks to being a seer. It's not all nightmares and doomsday warnings. As soon as I saw that rabbit, I knew what it was."

"Great," Val groaned. "Another know-it-all. Am I going to be the only one around here who doesn't have all the answers?"

*"You don't need the answers,"* Mister E said slyly. *"You just need to hit the things we tell you to hit."*

"Hardy har."

Gunter put a big hairy arm around her shoulders.

"It's OK, Val. We all have our rolls to play in this life. We don't all have to know everything. Some of us just have to look beautiful."

"Um." She looked up at the shaggy troll and found him posing like a runway model, bloody clothes and all. She sighed. "Sure. Whatever."

"That's the spirit. Now. Let's make like Alice and follow that rabbit!"

Val squealed as Gunter scooped her up without warning, deposited her on his massive shoulders and started running. Hanging on for dear life, she rode off on a troll, chasing a magic rabbit.

## 49

E ven by the standards of Val's life, this was weird. She was being carried by a troll, chasing a moon-rabbit with a tortured seer, who was in turn following a horde of goblins trying to escape with a magic staff. Oh, and there was a gay vampire in there somewhere too. Though where, exactly, Malcolm had gone, she wasn't sure. Wherever it was, he was being a lot stealthier than she, Gunter, and the rabbit brigade.

Which was in itself weird, now that she thought about it. Stealthy wasn't a word one would generally use when describing Malcolm.

Clinging to Gunter's shoulders, she shivered in the chill evening wind blowing from the bay. It carried the salty tang of the sea. The full moon had cleared the buildings now, illuminating the deserted streets with a silver light so bright it might have been day. Val could see the white rabbit a block ahead of them, its fur shining like a pale torch as it hopped after the goblins.

Val peered up at the moon, trying to gauge the time by how high the orb hung in the sky. How much time did they have left before the deadline? Could they retrieve the staff and get it back to the burial site before the clock struck midnight and the whole city turned into a blood-soaked pumpkin?

"Who am I kidding? I can't tell time by the moon. Hell, I can't even tell time by the sun, and it at least keeps regular hours," she grumbled. "Does anyone know what time it is?"

"It is time to retrieve the staff," Rosa said.

"Snark from you too?" Val asked. "Of us all, I would have thought at least you would be serious as a nightmare."

"As a nightmare?"

"Well, your nightmares are pretty serious, aren't they? Rivers of blood and all that."

"True. Though I was being serious. It is time to return the staff to its rightful place. Everything beyond that is immaterial."

"Yes, but..." Val decided to let it go. The conversation was going around in circles. Besides, Rosa was correct. It was time to end this.

They turned a corner and started to climb. There. At the top of the hill the mayor's mansion squatted behind manicured gardens, peering out over the city through tall lit windows. Beside it lurked an old stone church out of a movie set, complete with a crumbling graveyard. She could see the mass of goblins filing into the mansion's gardens through a wrought-iron gate, the stone staff held above their heads like a battle trophy.

"Faster!" She kicked her heels into her troll-steed.

"Hey!" Gunter growled. "None of that. Kick me again and you'll find yourself walking."

Val ignored him, already moving on to her next action. She called up her power, fingertips tingling with electricity, hair rising around her head in a waving halo of live strands. For once, she didn't have to worry about hitting anyone else; the goblins were a full block ahead of them. She could let her vengeance rip with impunity. She sucked up power until she couldn't hold another drop — until her skin felt stretched and tight, her body an overripe fruit ready to explode.

Then she called down the heavens.

Lightning sizzled out of the clear sky, turning the night into day, the thunderclap a titan's roar. It stabbed into the mass of goblins like a spear from the gods, flinging charred bodies everywhere it touched.

Val didn't have time to savor her success. They closed the distance to the charred goblins, and the sky began to cloud over. The air pressure dropped. She smelled rain. As fat drops began to fall, a dark form descended the front steps of the mayor's mansion.

The Rain King.

"Shit. Not this guy again," she snarled.

"Do not hurt him." Rosa clutched at her arm.

"Hurt him? I'm more worried about him hurting us."

The rain thickened as they approached the mansion, the air wavering through the curtains of water pouring down from the sky.

"Turn back," the Rain King intoned. "The time has come. You cannot stop it."

Val set her jaw.

"Can't I? Just watch me, buddy."

She reached back and hurled icy wind up the street, scattering the rain before her.

The tails of the Rain King's long coat blew back, but he was unmoved. He raised his hand and the rain redoubled, falling even more heavily, snuffing out Val's wind like a candle.

"You are too late," he said. "The time has come."

In the old church steeple, a deep bell began to toll. Midnight.

A pale, shining mist began to swirl as something stirred in the ancient graveyard. The soil boiled and churned. A decaying fist punched through the surface.

Val swore, her heart turning to ice in her chest.

The dead were rising.

# 50

The zombie rose to its feet, dirt cascading from decaying shoulders. Two rows over, another struggled to free itself from its grave. Then another.

Unlike in the movies, the zombies were completely silent.

"They probably don't have any vocal chords left," Val muttered.

One thing the movies did get right, though, was the shambling, lurching way they walked. Val knew this because the first had started to move toward her.

"Put me down." As Gunter set her on her feet, she raised her fists, ready for this new fight.

The troll put a hand on her shoulder.

"You get the staff," he said, brandishing his oversize wrench. "I'll handle the walking dead."

Val grimaced. Turning her back on a fight went against her every instinct.

But Gunter was right. The only way to end this was to return the staff to the burial chamber. If she did that, the dead would all go back where they belonged. The Rain King would too.

At least, that was what she hoped would happen. They were supposed to return the staff to the burial site before the dead rose. She didn't know if returning it after the fact would have the same effect. Or any effect. Maybe this was just the way the city would be from now on. Maybe Zombie Coffee would be overrun by a new, on-brand horde of clientele.

There was only one way to find out.

As she limped toward the staff, the rain intensified, sticking to her face in the now familiar way that nevertheless made panic rise. Not being able to breathe was terrifying, no matter how many times it happened to you.

She clenched her jaw and pushed, creating a small bubble of air around her face, keeping the water at bay.

The Rain King responded by redoubling his efforts. Water poured from the sky, driving her down to one knee. Val felt as if an entire waterfall was pounding her shoulders.

She grunted and tried to get back to her feet. She failed. The weight was too much for her wounded leg.

"I guess we're doing this the old-fashioned way then." Val began to crawl, struggling to move each limb forward, just a few inches at a time, mud sucking at her hands and knees as the weight of the world pressed down upon her back.

Rosa focused on her nephew.

"*Mi hijo*, don't do this. Please. This isn't you."

"*Tía?*"

The deluge slackened as the Rain King took an uncertain step forward.

Rosa moved to meet him. Tears streamed down her cheeks.

"Yes, Jorge. It's me. This isn't right. You are a good man."

"*Tía…*" The rain ceased falling entirely as he moved down the front walk.

Rosa smiled through her tears, stepping forward to meet him. His dark form towered over her as she wrapped her arms around his waist, pressing her cheek to his chest as she embraced him.

The Rain King's arms hung awkwardly at his sides. Hesitantly, he lifted one palm to pat Rosa's back.

Val groaned with relief, wiping her muddy hands on her soaked jeans as she staggered back to her feet. Now she just had to get the staff back where it belonged and the nightmare would be over.

She side-eyed the growing flock of zombies in the graveyard. The closest had almost reached Gunter, who waited for them, long wrench poised like a baseball bat in his hands. Hopefully, returning the staff would send them all back to their graves. If it didn't... well. One thing at a time.

As she was puzzling out how she was going to lift the cumbersome stone staff, the woman in the pink power suit stepped out onto the front porch of the mayor's mansion, her makeup and hair perfect as her voice rang in the chill night air.

"No. That's not the way this is going to go."

A wave of happiness swept over Val, causing the corners of her mouth to curl up into a goofy smile. The air around her felt soft and warm, like she was floating in a wet sauna. The colors of the world became vibrant and new, pulsing with life.

What was she doing again? She had no idea. It didn't matter anyway. Her mouth watered as she inhaled the rich scent of fresh-baked bread.

The woman in pink smiled. She was stunningly beautiful. The most perfect woman Val had ever seen.

"That's better. Now, why don't you go play with your new friends?"

Val turned and saw a group of welcoming people walking out of the graveyard. They carried picnic baskets and blankets. Her smile widened. This was going to be the best day ever.

"Sorry to ruin your fun." The old woman from the herb shop strode through the garden in a shaft of pale light, the Moon Rabbit cradled in her arms. The light smoothed away her wrinkles, making her appear young and strong again.

She gestured and the clouds parted, washing everything with the silver light of the full moon. The warmth drained from the world in an instant.

Val shook her head, suddenly dizzy. For the second time in five minutes, she had no idea what she had just been doing.

The pink woman's mouth pursed in an adorable pout.

"You are not welcome here, old woman. I did not invite you."

"No, you did not," the old woman agreed. She turned her wizened gaze toward Val. "But I owe this one a debt. As you know, we old gods take our debts seriously."

"A debt?" Val stared at her. As far as she knew, she hadn't done anything to put the old woman — or, as was now apparent, the Moon Goddess — in her debt.

"Yes, a debt. On the day you came to visit me, you saved a child from an angry mob. That child was my granddaughter. I now return the favor and release you from this woman's spell."

"You can't do that," the woman in pink shrieked. Her hair had come unpinned, wild strands writhing about her skull. Her once beautiful face transformed into a demonic mask of rage.

A knife appeared in her hand as she stepped toward the old woman

"Your time is over, crone. It's my time now." She raised the knife over her head, sharp tip glinting as she prepared to plunge it into the goddess's heart.

Val got there first.

"Not on my watch." She punched the succubus right in her pink face.

# 51

Val was expecting the pink woman to crumple. Or go flying. At the very least, she expected her to fall on her pink ass.

Unfortunately, the succubus did none of these things.

Val's fist hit her solidly in the face, snapping her head back. But other than that, the pink woman remained unmoved. She glared at Val, blood dripping from her split lip. She dabbed at it delicately with her manicured fingertips, her gaze turning murderous as she saw the red liquid on her skin.

"That," she growled, "was your last mistake."

The woman punched Val back. Hard.

The world spun as Val's body slammed into the wooden boards of the porch. Her ears rang as she woozily rose onto her elbows. She felt like she'd been hit with Gunter's wrench.

"What the hell?" she slurred. "How?"

*"She is a succubus,"* Mister E informed her. *"Even though the Moon Goddess may have broken her strongest power — her charm — she still packs quite the punch. Succubi leech energy from those under their thrall. She's obviously been feeding off the mayor and his staff for quite some time, as well as the crowds at all those rabble-rousing speeches. I'd guess she's stored up quite the reserve of power by now."*

"You think?" Val scrambled back as the pink woman stepped toward her. She needed to stay out of reach. Another punch like that might snap her neck.

With the Moon Goddess's light washing away the succubus's charm power, the pink woman's true features were revealed. Much like the fae when you removed their glamour, her true face was anything but beautiful. Her eyes were thin slashes with vertical reptilian pupils. Her elongated jaw hinged open like a snake's, revealing rows of circular, lamprey-like teeth.

"You can't stop me," she hissed.

Val hit the succubus with a fist of wind but the pink woman just leaned into it, shrugging the blow aside like a tanker ship plowing through a small wave. Val tried to scuttle away, but the woman's hand shot out snake-fast, latching on to her ankle and jerking her to a halt. She lifted Val into the air by her leg, effortlessly dangling her upside down.

"You are nothing." She tossed Val aside like a piece of trash.

Val's world became an out-of-control merry-go-round, spinning wildly as she flew through the air. Then she abruptly stopped spinning, the motion replaced by pain as she slammed into one of the porch's massive faux-classical support pillars. She felt something snap inside her torso and every breath became a sharp stab. A rib broken, at least. Maybe two.

She looked up through a haze of pain as the succubus bore down on her, unable to do more than whimper. Her entire body felt like one big bruise. Each breath was agony.

The pink woman stood over her, triumphant, basking in the moment as she prepared to deliver the coup de grace.

"This city is mine." She opened her horrible mouth wide, saliva dripping from her circular teeth as she leaned in. Val tried to gather her power, but the pain broke her concentration, magic slipping like sand through her fingers.

Despair filled her. So this was how it ended.

She felt an unexpected twinge of relief at the thought. She carried so much guilt and anguish. So many people she cared about were dead in the ground. She had fought so hard. She was beyond tired. Finally, she could lay down her burden and rest.

Val closed her eyes.

"No. This city is not yours. It is mine," the Rain King said.

Rain hammered down, soaking Val instantly. The deluge wasn't focused on her, but even the spray was like a jackhammer pounding. It went on far too long.

When the rain finally eased up, she opened her eyes.

The woman in pink was gone. Only the Rain King remained, his dark shadow stretching across the porch like an accusatory finger.

Both relief and disappointment flooded Val, along with a fresh twinge of guilt. The Rain King had saved her. Apparently, she couldn't even die right.

"Where is she?" she croaked, wincing as her broken ribs stabbed into her.

"She is gone," the Rain King said simply.

"Dead?"

"Gone," he repeated. "She will not return to my city."

"Your city," she whispered.

Val had been starting to think of it as her city. But of course, that couldn't be true. The city was too big to belong to her. Or she was too small. Either way, it made sense for it to be the Rain King's city now. He was a god, after all.

Her gaze drifted over to the Moon Goddess, still cradling the shining rabbit. Gods controlled cities. Not little witches. She'd been stupid to think that she might be able to make a difference.

"Not stupid, child," the Moon Goddess said. "You are still needed."

"Needed?" Val scoffed a laugh, then instantly regretted it, wincing as her ribs stabbed inside her. She continued in a pained whisper. "I didn't do anything here. You and the Rain King did all the work."

"On the contrary. You brought us all together at the proper time and place. The Rain King could not vanquish the succubus while he remained under her thrall. My power was needed to free him. You brought me into the equation when you saved my granddaughter from the mob in the street. You are the thread that binds us all together. None of this would have happened if it weren't for you."

Val grimaced.

"But I didn't do any of that intentionally. It just happened."

"Good happens when good people take action. Often the results of those actions are things we do not intend. They are often things we do not even see. Butterfly wings of causality, rippling out through the world. Even if you do not see the direct results of your goodness, Val Keri, never doubt that they exist. You are like a warm breeze, stirring many things into motion. That is your true role in this world. You do more good than you will ever know."

Val felt a tear drip from her chin and was surprised to discover that she was crying.

"It doesn't feel that way," she whispered. "It hurts."

"I know, child. Your burden is great. But know that it is only given to you because you have the strength to bear it," the Moon Goddess said gently. Then she turned her gaze toward the graveyard, where Gunter stood clutching his wrench, facing a shuffling tide of zombies. "Now, I think it is time to end this. Don't you?"

## 52

"We should really get goddesses on our side more often," Gunter said.

"Cheers to that," Val agreed, clinking glasses with him.

She watched enviously as the troll took a long swallow of his beer. Val missed beer. She did not, however, miss the raging alcoholic version of herself who used to drink it. So she took a long drink of her ginger beer instead. Which was still festive, in its own way.

She looked around at the common area of the Imaginarium, filled with people smiling and chatting. As if the city hadn't nearly been overrun by zombies just a few days ago. Most of them had no idea how close they'd come to disaster.

Preventing the zombie apocalypse had turned out easier than Val had expected. Having a goddess on your side was like having a cosmic sized can of WD-40 and a roll of duct tape. You could fix just about anything.

The Moon Goddess had transported them back to the native burial site, and they returned the stone staff to its rightful place inside the bone-lined chamber where they had found Jorge's body. Val then called down the mother of all lightning storms to collapse the tunnel, burying the entrance to the chamber beneath tons of rock and hopefully ensuring the staff would never be disturbed again. For good measure, the Rain King summoned a deluge that caused a mudslide over the rubble, burying it even further.

Yes, the Rain King was still around. To Val's surprise, he hadn't disappeared when they returned the staff to the burial chamber. It seemed he was a permanent fixture in the city now. Val had mixed feelings about him sticking around, given how many times he had attempted to drown her, but at least the Rain King wasn't under the control of the mayor's flunkies anymore, so that had to be an improvement. She hoped.

Actually, if anything was going to keep him human, it was Rosa.

As if the thought had summoned her, Rosa materialized out of the crowd. Val smiled at her friend.

"You look better. Like you might even be sleeping through the night sometimes."

Rosa returned the smile. "I haven't woken up screaming in days. You have no idea how amazing it is to wake up to the sunrise instead of nightmare visions in the dark."

Rosa was still gaunt and she still had bags under her eyes, but they were slowly fading. Val hoped Rosa's dark premonitions had left her for good, though she had her doubts. Fae gifts were more persistent than poison oak. And even less pleasant.

"Have you seen Jorge?"

"The Rain King," Rosa corrected somberly. "Jorge is gone. He died in that burial chamber. The Rain King is someone else. There are traces of Jorge in there, but he's become a different person. He's the Rain King now."

"I'm sorry."

"Me too." Rosa sighed. "I'm trying to accept the change philosophically. I mean, that's life, isn't it? Nothing stays the same. People evolve. The old you dies, and a new you rises from the ashes. Sometimes we evolve by choice, sometimes evolution is thrust upon us and we have to adapt to it as best we can. I'm certainly not the same person I was a month ago. Neither is he."

"That's a very mature view of things."

Rosa laughed.

"I'm trying. Seers are supposed to be wise, aren't they? I figure I need to absorb a bit of philosophy so I can make cryptic pronouncements about the future."

Val laughed too. She was impressed. Rosa seemed to have come through her ordeal not only intact, but with a new outlook on life. Apparently, some people used their trauma to become better people. Who knew?

"Do you believe the statement the mayor released?" Val asked.

"Do I believe that Mayor Light was completely under the sway of the succubus and in no way responsible for his own actions?" Rosa rolled her eyes. "No. I believe he's a hateful, bigoted piece of shit who is trying to weasel his way out of the consequences of his actions."

Val sighed.

"Yeah, you're probably right. Though part of me still wants to believe that things will get better now that she's out of the picture."

"Hope springs eternal."

"It has to, doesn't it? I mean, if we don't have hope, then we've got nothing, really." The crowd swirled and Val smiled as she caught sight of Sandra. "Speaking of hope."

The hooded gorgon stood next to the Librarian, who radiated power despite appearing to be a small, mousy woman with glasses and holes in the elbows of her cardigan.

*"Strange attraction spreads it wings,"* Mister E said. He looked suitably festive with his top hat and long cigarette holder.

Val raised an eyebrow at him.

"Did you just quote The Cure?"

*"Why wouldn't I? I live inside you. I listened to all the music you did growing up. I happen to like The Cure. You should listen to them more often."*

Val shook her head.

Malcolm swung into view, wearing a sparkling tiara. The birthday boy was in his element, glowing under all the attention. He smiled when he saw Val.

"I think I might need to have birthdays more often. This is too much fun to only happen once a year. Once a month would be better. I could even have one weekly!"

"Are you sure you want to do that?" Val asked. "If your birthday was every week, think of how fast you'd age. You'd be an ancient crone in no time. We'd have to replace your tiara with a witch hat."

"You are not touching my tiara. Don't even think about it." Malcolm clutched the tiara protectively. "Also, you're overlooking a very important fact. I'm immortal now. Nobody cares how old a vampire is. In fact, we creatures of the night get sexier over time. A five-hundred-year-old vampire is infinitely more fascinating than a fifty-year-old."

She had to admit, he had her there.

"Fine. But we are not throwing a party every week. Weekly birthdays are also infinitely less special than annual ones."

"Party pooper," Malcolm pouted.

"What happened to you at the mayor's mansion, anyway? I didn't see you helping during the final showdown," she asked, raising an eyebrow at Malcolm.

"Ah, well. I was wrestling with the goblins and they sort of..." he looked away, his voice trailing off into an inaudible mumble.

"What was that?"

"They sat on me, ok? A bunch of the little fuckers piled on top of me until I couldn't move and then they just sat there."

Val and Rosa exchanged glances. Together they burst out laughing.

Malcolm changed the subject.

"Have you seen Hillary? I heard this shindig was all her idea, but I haven't seen her yet."

Val frowned. "No, I haven't. She's been strangely absent the last couple of weeks. I hope she's all right."

"I'm sure she's fine. She gets like that sometimes." Malcolm waved away her concern. "She needs her alone time. She'll come back around when she's feeling social again. Still, I would like to thank her for all this. Let me know if you see her."

"Will do."

Despite Malcolm's glib explanation, Val had a feeling there might be more to Hillary's absence than he thought. Although she had to admit that maybe being a private investigator was simply making her suspicious of everything. Still, she'd try to keep an eye on Hillary. The last thing she needed was a housemate in some kind of trouble. Again.

"Stop scowling," Rosa said, threading her arm through Val's. "Whatever it is that you're worrying about, it isn't here and it isn't now. Right now you're at a party, surrounded by friends. It's OK to loosen up. Be here now. Let the weight of the world off your shoulders for a while. I think you've earned it. We all have."

Val nodded. It was good advice. Be here now. Put her past regrets aside. Set down her fears for the future. Exist only here, in this moment.

Such a simple thing.

Yet it often felt like the hardest thing in the world to do.

Still, she would try.

Val Keri took a sip of her ginger beer and looked around at a party filled with those she cared about most in the world. She breathed it all in. Then she breathed it out and stepped forward, into the present.

<<<<>>>>

Thank you so much for reading Black rain. I hope you enjoyed reading it as much as I enjoyed writing it.

Before you go, please take a moment to leave a review. Even just some stars or a few words can make a huge difference in helping other readers discover the world of The Keri Chronicles.

Thank you very much.

Yours,
A.C. Arquin

# GET YOUR FREE STORY!

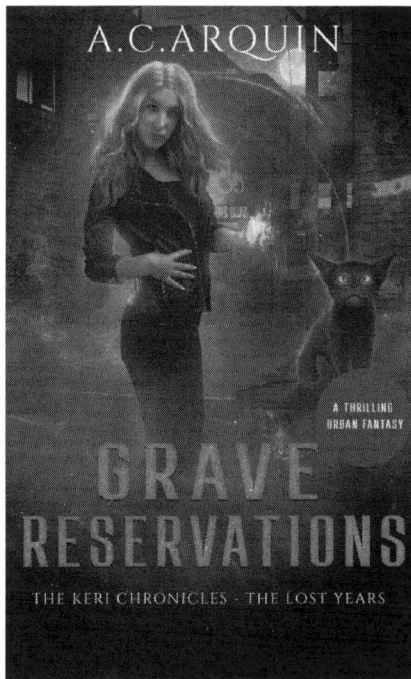

*Join the Arquinworlds Reader Group to get your free story from The Keri Chronicles - The Lost Years! Go to www.arquinworlds.com.*

# ABOUT THE AUTHOR

A.C. Arquin lives in his own worlds. At least, that's what his teachers always told him when they caught him reading a book in class instead of paying attention to the lesson.

Now all grown up, he still prefers realms of imagination to reality. The only difference is that nowadays, he writes down his adventures and shares them with the world.

When not writing, he is also a very busy audiobook narrator, under the name J.S. Arquin.

Get a FREE KERI CHRONICLES PREQUEL STORY as well, as all the latest news and deals, by joining his Reader's Group at www.arquinworlds.com/

**f 𝕏 ⓘ**

# BOOKS BY A.C. ARQUIN

THE KERI CHRONICLES

Dead Wrong

Pale Midnight

Twilight Storm

Jade Secrets

Black Rain

Grave Reservations (Val Keri, The Lost Years)

THE CRIMSON DUST CYCLE (A Dystopian Space Adventure. Published as J.S. Arquin)

Ascent (Book 1)

Slide (Book 2)

Peak (Book 3)

Twist (A Crimson Dust Prequel)

The Crimson Dust Cycle Box Set

OTHER BOOKS

The Itch (A Stand-Alone Gaslamp Fantasy Thriller)

Printed in Dunstable, United Kingdom